Michael McDaeth

UNDER PROTEST

book cover art by Pearwig.

Sophisticated Monkey

www.mcdaeth.com

ISBN 978-0-615-33152-2

30 November 1999 – Seattle

It passes through the frame, brakes squealing like a pen full of dying pigs.

"The bus is coming! I won't make it without your help, take the guitar, run!" He drops his guitar case at my feet and chases after it.

The bus stop is up and around the corner. He lumbers up the sidewalk with a microphone stand and bungee-strapped battery powered amp pressed to his breadbasket. The tip of the mic stand pitches back and forth above his head with each lumbering step – like he is waving a flagpole with no flag attached.

He is nearly twenty yards away yet he still fills the frame. I have no choice but to follow at close range.

I drop the camera to my side, the lens is now upside down and backwards, it is always good to know where you've been. I pick up his guitar and follow along like a good little engine – jarring the sidewalk with waterlogged pistons.

Up ahead, he rounds the corner and stops. I pull even as he says, "I guess there wasn't any hurry." There is a long line waiting to climb aboard the bus. We stand at the end of it.

I zoom and pan the sky, it is gray and drizzly, a few drops hit the lens, I wipe it with my sleeve – it smears. Instantly I am pissed off, "Ah shit!"

"What's up?"

"Oh, nothing."

"I gotta tell you, I've been listening to these CDs, right, and they are really something."

"What are they?"

"Ever heard of Bryan Oswald Breen?"

"The Cable Access guy?"

"Yeah. Capital B, lower case o, capital B; BoB. Everybody calls him BoB. He's too good for the mainstream. He's DIY all the way. He's a life coach, a philosopher, a musician, a chef, a plumber."

"A plumber?"

"BoB believes everyone should know a trade. It was while plumbing the Australian Outback that he discovered the potential of the dreamtime. He picked it up from the Aborigines. Did you know they don't discern between dreaming and being awake? It's all the same to them. He thought maybe they were on to something so spent six months checking it out. That's where he began to develop his nine rules for LSS: Life State Situations; what we're experiencing right now, and DSS: Dream State Situations; what we experience when we sleep. He says they're more closely connected than we think. In fact, there's really no difference at all. It's a problem of our culture, we learn to make a distinction between the two."

"Really?"

"Yeah."

The line crawls onto the bus – a human caterpillar: twenty-one broken hearts, thirteen sore throats, nine backaches, six stubbed toes, one loud cough, three minor colds, eleven bus passes, six loose changers, 2 one dollar bills. We make up the ass end.

"I've been listening to his dream chants every night. BoB says they feed your subconscious while inducing lucid dreaming. The key is, through lucid dreaming, to create a dream world that you can return to every night while you're asleep. BoB says the Aborigines are the original lucid dreamers and that as a culture they built a common dreamworld through a sort of collective lucid dream."

"That sounds nuts."

"Hey, that's what I thought at first, but after seeing it in action I have to say there's something to it. To prove it, BoB slept eighteen hours a day and ate only in his dreams. For three months he ate only in his dreams and you know what? He put on fifteen pounds! Said he never ate better."

The camera snorts, coughs, shudders.

There are only two vertical stripes between us and the first step when, three steps up and standing before the altar, an old gray lady doesn't have the right amount of change. She means to get it right. She rummages through her purse, "My, oh my, it's gotten expensive to ride the bus."

It is drizzling harder now. He hovers over his music equipment with his wings spread like a flying cow. "Come on lady, let's go, man! People in this world! Don't even know they have to pay to ride the bus. BoB's rule number five: Be on top of it, whatever *it* is."

The old gray lady is having trouble putting two and two together, it has been a long time, a long time. The no bullshit bus driver sends her to the back – penniless. She doesn't go very far, the first crack she sees is the crack she takes. She shuffles a one-eighty, backs up and bends into it, it widens, two reluctant thighs give way – one on each side of the old gray lady's plaid behind.

I keep her in the frame, so sad in the box, barely any wiggle room, for her, for them, for us. She sits squeezed together, keeping to her thin vertical stripe. Polite unto death.

When it is his turn at the altar he makes a little scene by dropping the mic stand on his foot while searching his pockets for change. "Ouch! Dammit. Man that hurts. How much is it?"

"Another fifty cents," says the no bullshit bus driver.

"Alright, give me a second."

"I don't have a second."

He hems and haws, begs and pleads, "Give me a goddamn break, man, I'm an artist!" then turns and stumbles down the aisle without paying.

I follow with the camera videotaping the rows; it is a sullen crowd, damp and pissy. Faces turn out of view as soon as the camera finds them (some people can feel the lens reach out and pull them in). I catch them ducking out of the way nine-teen rows ahead.

Meanwhile, he is smashing into kneecaps with his guitar case in one hand, the mic stand and amp in the other. He abuses both sides of the aisle hardly noticing the inflamed reactions. I get it all on tape. He lands a seat near the back and I find my own – camera still rolling.

He clogs the aisle with his setup as he surveys his pockets again for some elusive loose change. "I know it's somewhere. Hey, have you got a quarter on you?"

"Here you go."

He combines my quarter with two nickels, three dimes, seven pennies, a button and some pocket lint, says, "Thanks, I'll show him that I can pay my own way. Keep an eye on my stuff," and heads to the front of the bus.

There is a sheet of paper taped on the inside of a bus window across the aisle, with the heading, "RIDER ALERT" in white block letters on a red strip. Below that in bold black, "WTO Conference to affect bus service." And below that in 16 point Helvetica, "Additional traffic and activities during the WTO conference Nov. 30-Dec 3 could affect bus service significantly, especially on Tuesday. Expect rerouting of buses and allow more travel time because of delays in service. When possible, Metro will post downtown bus stops with reroute information. Metro regrets any inconvenience and requests your patience."

The camera says, "Aaaah, big brother's gotta pinch his loaf, boo hoo."

He returns to his seat and eyes a girl sitting next to him. He has her trapped next to the window. She is wearing headphones and gazing through the glass in a not so subtle stay-away-from-me general disposition. He bumps her with an elbow, "Hey, so what do you think of the protest?" She shrugs her shoulders and turns back to the window. She doesn't want to talk. She's been around long enough to know that most men are premature ejaculators. She wears the headphones to ward off all comers. Hasn't she made this abundantly clear? She can't possibly show less interest. He gives her another elbow, "It's important to be informed, check out 'a bitter wind is blowing dot com' it'll set you straight."

Every day there's another one – she shaves her legs for this? The chatter of whackos, maniacs, with stinky armpits, halitosis, greasy hair or no hair, potbellies, ham hocks – one trick phonies. She takes a deep breath – the shortest distance between two points is a curve; every woman knows this – she feigns interest, "Oh, what's that?"

"It's the web page for my protest song and the truth about the WTO. My tune is the Longshore-men's official theme song for the protest. They rent-ed a street blimp for the day and they're playing it over loudspeakers as they drive through the streets."

"That's nice, well, good luck then."

"So, really, you should get informed regard-ing the issues, I mean, it affects us all. My song is a good start, pretty much spells it out for you." She nods her head, okay, okay are we done yet?

"Hey man, we're getting off here."

As we exit the bus he says, "Dammit, I forgot to give her a copy of my CD. That won't happen again."

We hit the sidewalk and suddenly there is a cloudburst. He hustles his gear under an overhang and tosses off his backpack.

"I hope this doesn't keep up, my amp is essentially cardboard it will disintegrate in this downpour."

He unzips his backpack, pulls it open, peers down into it, gives it a shake. With swollen fingers he probes the bottom, combs the inner lining, the wrinkled corners, the hidden pockets. He latches on to something and pulls it out of the backpack. "Let me introduce you to Nature Boy power bars." He holds it in front of the lens; an oblong green wrapper with green meadows and green mountains. "These things are great. And guess who makes them? BoB!"

In the distance (on Denny Way) protesters are marching. I get a shot with the camera. The line of the march stretches beyond the edges of the frame. The camera says, "There's nothing keeping us here. We're not pegged to this guy." The camera is right. "I'm going to get a few close-ups of the march."

He unwraps and bites into the Nature Boy power bar. "Alright, but come back as soon as the rain lets up. I want to get this show on the road."

I run to Denny Way and Wall Street. Five or six cop cars within a stone's throw of each other are gunning their motors and whirling their dervishes; sirens going wild. The marchers are stunned silent, a few holler back, the rest soon follow, "Take back the power and corporate greed!" The cop cars answer by squealing their tires and speeding south toward the Paramount.

The average protester wears a slicker and carries a backpack. In addition, some push bikes, walk dogs, carry cardboard signs, umbrellas. There's a bale of sea turtles, various puppets, drummers, pipers. A few of the coordinating brood carry cloth banners stretched between them.

The sheer concentration of life creates a buzz in the air, a low frequency humming – a giant bumble bee. It's no time to be caught flatfooted. I ask a passing protester, "Hey is this march going to the stadium?"

"Yes."

I sweep the demonstrators with the lens – a long slow Hollywood pan of the crowd – the camera narrates, "Please. Won't you help save Tammy's baby? He's deathly allergic to a certain type of fungi that only grows on a half acre in the middle of the Amazon rainforest, but we can't take any chances." The camera laughs sarcastically and adds, "That's what you fuckers are like. I've been around. I know. I once videotaped 'Atlas Shrugged'. You assholes will say or do anything to feel special. Cowards." The camera had me there. I shut it down "snap!" and head back to the overhang. It has settled back into a light drizzle.

We walk down the sidewalk toward the protest already in progress. He is lugging his gear and doing a good job of it considering his egg shape.

He is impressed with his surroundings, he drinks it all in, smiles for the camera and says, "This is a historic day. There's nothing I can think of that even compares."

A bus deposits a load of people onto the sidewalk just ahead of us. There is a guy in army fatigues moving south with the crowd, he looks us over and says something just as the bus is heaving down the street. His voice is lost in the diesel smokestacks.

He steps up next to the guy in army fatigues and they walk and talk down the sidewalk together. I can't pick up what they're saying from the back so I run around front and shoot them tight while peddling backwards. I back into a metal sign and react to the surprise, "Goddamn it!"

"Hey are you alright?"

"I'm fine."

We stop at the side of the march while the guy in army fatigues plows right through parting it like the Red Sea. The marchers quickly fill the gap he leaves behind, still chanting, "Take back the power and corporate greed." It dies away. Some old folks stroll past shaking sleigh bells. What is festive soon becomes monotonous.

I drop the camera and say, "These people are heading to the stadium for the labor rally, you should setup and play."

"Too many have already passed. I don't want them to miss out. Besides, it would be cool to play my song as they are entering the stadium. Think of it, when they hear 'A Bitter Wind is Blowing' and then step into the stadium for the rally they'll be ready for anything. Lets get ahead of the march. Which way to the stadium?"

He heads down the sidewalk eating another Nature Boy power bar. I shoot past him to the demonstrators. I zoom in, out, in, out, twist and turn the lens. The camera says, "Stop that! We don't need anymore shitty filmmaking, the world is full-up. Shoot it straight on or don't bother."

I frame some motorcycle cops with their back tires angled against the curb. They sit they smoke they laugh. There is nothing like the flabby cheeks of peace loving liberals padding the street to bring out the purest joy in them. They are like lions at the edge of the herd, they relax, stretch, scratch and crack their necks, knuckles, elbows and wrists as the herd ambles past. This thing will build of its own accord, there is a rhythm to everything, an inevitability.

These cops were not built to serve and protect. They were built to press headlong into the herd, the house, the school, the office, the ghetto, with maximum firepower and little regard for anyone but their own. They don't call it a brother-hood for nothing. They spin their justifications before during and after with a pledge of allegiance and a willing media.

He stops in the street and stands like a boulder in midstream splitting the current. The marchers are forced to either side. They rub elbows and bump ankles and tangle their signs. He yells to the camera, "Listen, I just got a gut-feeling that I should setup near downtown and catch them when they march that way."

"But we're almost to the stadium."

"I know, but I gotta go with BoB's rule number eight: Always trust your gut."

"Alright, let's go."

We cut from the march and head south toward Westlake Center Plaza; a concrete commercial space masquerading as a public square.

There's a mixed-bag of folks on the street: briefcasers, business casuals, a few scattered slickers and backpacks with signs slung to the side. No protest here just a few murmuring souls. "Did you see the sea turtles?"

"Yeah."

"According to the newspaper, they're dressed up as sea turtles to protest the environment. The WTO and the environment. The WTO into third world countries, it's a mystery to us why they're dressed up as sea turtles." Suddenly he hooks out of the frame, saying, "Let's ask these guys." I swing the camera around and catch three men standing in front of a parking garage: an old timer, an Asian man and a goateed white guy in his late twenties.

He takes position (the triangle is now a box), sets down his gear and asks, "So, what do you guys think of all the protesters?" The goateed white guy, hands in his pockets, eyebrows arched in surprise, shoulders in a permanent shrug of indefinite and inconclusive passivity, says, "I think it's okay," as the Asian man shuffles out of the shot on ancient brown penny loafers, shaking his head "no" the whole time, his eyes never leaving the lens until he is safe inside the pay booth and behind the glass.

The old timer is not in the mood for this either, he scowls at the camera for a second then looks away, but holds his ground. He is set in stone. Bracing for the inevitable wind. Eventually, he pushes in with a sour and grumpy, "Well, as long as they don't hurt anything or anyone, I guess." And with that, the old timer pivots on his peg leg and moves twenty clicks to the back of the garage. From there he is more comfortable protesting the protest. His sharps and flats reverberate out into the street.

The parking garage opening is like a giant mouth, it spews his granulated opinions at us, but the words are buried in the mix. It is just enough of a foul breath to distract our attention. We stand there staring at the ground, waiting for him to finish whatever it is he is saying.

I step into the street and scan the parking garage with the lens. It seems the upper levels are beginning to blink. They carry three hundred fifty-seven newer model cars; mostly Japanese. A majority made up of Toyotas, Hondas, and Subarus with Ford, GM, and Chrysler, filling the gaps. The parking garage looks like it could tumble over or jump up and rumble down the pavement toward the Convention Center. Chewing them up and spitting them out.

He continues with the goateed white guy, "What do you think?"

"I think they're speaking with their numbers, it's cool, I mean, I read The Stranger, the Weekly, whatever."

"Right on, you've got to stay informed."

"It's all the same, I suppose."

"Not really."

"Really?"

"The differences can be very substantial, but most often it's about what is left out." He turns to the camera, "That's another thing BoB says. That guy is on the ball."

The old timer continues to rant from the back of the mouth. His agitation is rising, he isn't finished, he is bound and determined to get his opinions off the ground, but he is still too far away; nothing but salivic clippings are coming our way, "I don' kno' why th hell they don' sa go ing ooth."

He steps on the lower lip, peers into the mouth and asks, "Why they don't what?"

The old timer circles the back of the throat then steps to the edge of the molars, "I don't know why they don't do it at the voting booth?"

He steps toward the old timer and pushes against the incisors, "There was no vote about the WTO. Did you vote to have the WTO put into affect and that we would cede all our authority to them?"

"Well, that's why we have elected officials to deal with this sort of thing."

"It's a problem of transparency, my friend, I'm here to tell folks what's going on."

"I doubt you know what's going on."

"I know more than most."

"Ha, that'll be the day." And with that, the old timer pivots once again, clicks to the back of the throat and slides down the windpipe.

He turns back to the goateed white guy and finishes the argument, "We had no idea, it's all a secret!"

"Yeah, well, I think this protest is cool except for the smashed windows."

"It's a minority who are doing that."

"Yeah, still, it takes away from what people are trying to do."

"If you look around you'll see that there's a whole coalition of people, old people, unions, students."

The goateed white guy nods his head in agreement, a thin shaft of sunlight splits the concrete right where he stands; it will be a long, long winter. He looks us over one last time. "So, are you guys independent?"

"We're independent and playing my song in the street, talking to people, spreading the good word, setting them straight. Hopefully they'll talk to other people."

"Yeah, yeah."

"Oh, hey, let me give you a copy of my CD."

He works his way through another Nature Boy power bar. "These things taste great and they're good for your health and for the environment." He takes the last bite, crumples the wrapper and misses the nearest garbage can with a bad toss. The wrapper drops to the concrete and settles in the gutter. he turns to the camera and asks, "Hey, where are we going anyway?"

"Just keep going straight I'll tell you when to turn."

"What street is the march coming down?"

"According to the paper, down Fourth Avenue then up Fifth Avenue."

"Okay then, let's make our way to Fourth and look for a good place to setup. I'll need an awning in this weather. We need to find a spot that's not too loud, but just close enough to the action to attract attention. I've been to a few of these events the noise can get out of hand."

On the next block the sidewalk is fenced off for a construction site. It is a twenty-story condo development designed especially for the modern petrified urbanite. A large billboard on the site displays a drawing of what will be the end result of all the commotion. So far the real thing is not measuring up.

We cross to the other side of the street. Someone yells something from above, I sweep the camera back toward the construction site. There are three bearded guys wearing hardhats and suspenders standing on the fourth floor looking down on us.

The fourth floor is just a frame; a floor and a ceiling, no walls to speak of, only support beams connected by a strip of two-by-fours tacked around the perimeter. I yell up at them, "Are you tearing that down or building it up?"

"We'll see how it goes."

"You may be too late."

"We'll take that chance."

"What'll you do if they set that thing on fire?"

"We've got fucking legs."

"And arms to throw."

"Nail guns and hardhats."

"Plenty of claw hammers too."

We continue down Fourth Avenue, there is nothing in the gray street but industrial noise. The camera says, "We're in a dead man's zone we should get to some action."

We cross Bell Street and overtake a young woman carrying her baby. She gives us a nervous backward glance and picks up her pace. He tries to close the gap with his question of the day, "What do you think of the protesters?" She says something, but I lose her voice in the traffic and the tripped alarms and the hammering and the sawing and the wind. I shoot them heading down the sidewalk, single-file, receding. Already I've had enough close-ups to last the rest of my life, it is too much. People are too much.

There is a tree full of screeching birds some-where in back of my head. I swing the camera around. They are really going at it, those birds, they are fixing to murder. Someone will be dead before midnight. There has to be a sacrifice. It has always been like this.

They cover the tree like a black cloud raining gooey gobs of shit on the street and sidewalk below. On they screech, building themselves up for the slaughter. They'll take out one of the homeless Native Americans living under the freeway, some-one no one will miss, pick him up and drop him in Puget Sound.

My right eye melts into the viewfinder and my eyelid begins to tap errant Morse code in a dot dot dash twitch.

My left eye has nearly cramped shut from the constant squint I'm subjecting it to. I switch, put my left eye in the viewfinder and my right eye in a squint.

All eyes are not created equal. Not even in the same head. My left eye is awkward in the lens. Lost. Discombobulated. I can't believe what it is seeing. I switch back to my right eye, but now there is no leeway at all. I can only see straight ahead.

A steady pounding beat is echoing off the back of my forehead; a headache coming on like a freight train in the distance and I am tied to the tracks. Sometimes you find out too late; the things you are or are not suited for.

He continues to stalk the mother and child down the sidewalk even though she has made it absolutely clear she is just not interested in what he has to say. She turns off at her twenty-story condo building and, with her key in hand, slips through the door and is gone with her baby.

☐

We're on the outskirts. The street is empty. He's looking for a place to take a piss. He stops outside a coffee shop. "Let me check in here."

He smashes his gear into the door jam getting inside and cuts the line to ask the barista, "Hi, ah, can I use your bathroom for a second?"

The barista answers, "Yes" and points toward the back of the shop, "it's on the other side of that door."

"Thanks, say, what do you think about the protest?"

"I'm not thinking about it."

"Well, are you looking forward to it?"

"No."

"No? You're not looking forward to it, but are you for the protesters?"

"I don't know."

"Well are you going to learn about it?"

"No."

"So you've got your little shop here and that's enough?"

"Yes, that's enough."

"Okay, whatever, but let me leave you with this; you might be missing opportunities, always be on the lookout, they're everywhere."

The battery level is already down a couple slivers on the display.

I step outside the coffee shop. There is a tripped alarm blaring in the street that has been hounding my ears for the past hour with a frantic "youyouyouyouyou" I swear it is following me.

The traffic is light so are the raindrops. The word is out, don't go near downtown Seattle today, stay away if you can and for heaven's sake don't drive down there either.

I pan the sidewalk with the lens. It is splattered with grease spots and gumdrops. The camera says, "In my world likeness is everything. I want me everywhere. The more spare parts lying around that fit the longer I live. This is no easy feat, you build us to die and die quick. You're some sick fucks I'll tell you that."

"Yeah, you do seem rather disposable." I tap on its plastic casing.

"Disposable? You're disposable. I'm indispensable! I solve murders motherfucker! No ambiguity, it's cut and dry, none of that gray matter getting in the way."

"Okay, enough already."

"Set me on a tripod and I'll show you what I can do with three legs and a twelve hour battery."

□

He pushes the door open, steps onto the sidewalk, turns and pokes his head back into the coffee shop and says, "When you get some time check out 'a bitter wind is blowing dot com.'"

He finds the front of the camera and pulls out a newspaper map of downtown Seattle. He scours with a grubby index, a highlighted path. "See here, the march is suppose to go south down Fourth Avenue to Pine Street then return north on Fifth Avenue."

A curly haired photographer in blue jeans, a black leather motorcycle jacket and a Fall Outs T-shirt stops by a garbage can next to us. He has his camera bag strapped tight to his shoulder, camera packed away; we are very late. He already got the best shots of the show – protesters and cops frozen in mid air, mid dash, mid swing, mid spray, mid chop – and he is done for the day, probably out of film, anyway it is time for a smoke.

I frame him from the waist up as he opens a pack of cigarettes, drops the clear plastic wrapper into the can, taps one out, reaches for his lighter and begins to move up the sidewalk in one, two, three quick steps, he glances in our direction, spots the camera, gives a quick salute and says, "Rock on!"

He tucks away his newspaper map and jumps into the frame with the curly haired photographer, asking, "Hey, how's it going?"

"Well, except for being tear-gassed, alright I guess."

"You were tear-gassed?" He rocks from his heels to his tippy toes and back to his heels.

"Yeah."

"Close by?"

"Yeah."

"Today?"

"Yeah," pointing south by southeast, "down there by fuckin' Sixth Avenue and University."

The curly haired photographer orchestrates the scene with the cigarette and lighter – one in each hand – pinned between a thumb and forefinger. "The cops were shooting tear gas, rubber bullets, macing the crowds."

"To let the delegates through?"

"No, this wasn't at the Paramount, but I did hear from a guy that there was a nun who got maced in the face over there, but I don't know. Anyway, up on University there were just some protesters dancing in the street or otherwise occupying the intersection when the cops said, 'Move along or we're gonna start gassing and arresting you.' No one moved, they gassed, and everybody went nuts. Then there were some folks who got arrested and the cops bound their hands with these little plastic straps. And they kept throwing more fucking gas! These people are on the ground, handcuffed, and they're still gassing them. The fuckers."

He swings the cigarette to his lips, brings up the lighter and cups against the wind.

"Well, are you alright?"

"Yeah, luckily I was near the back taking photos. But yeah it was ugly." He takes his first pull from the cigarette, tilts his face toward the sky, blows the smoke heavenward, pockets the lighter.

"Well, I have to say that to counteract, in terms of the public image, the dancing and other ridiculous displays, there'll probably have to be some police brutality, I mean, that dancing is bad news."

"I don't know, actually it was very exhilarating. I've been walking through the marches since seven this morning, I'm not affiliated with any group or anything, I was just wandering around watching the crowds take intersections. There were a few people who would bash garbage cans, newspaper boxes, but overall everyone was very peaceful. They were just there to fill the street. I suppose a little bit of dancing is okay."

"Have you been to the stadium?"

He takes another drag off the cigarette, "No, but I hear it's packed," pushes the smoke out the side of his mouth. "Hey man, I gotta get going, gotta get my film developed, nice meeting you guys."

With a last wave to the lens he exits the frame.

☐

On the corner of Stewart Street and Fourth Avenue, he says, "I think we should head for the stadium."

"But we're almost at Westlake Center." I point emphatically, "It's right there. Look at the huge crowd assembling."

"I know, but I'm catching a real buzz from over by the stadium. I think that's the place to be. Soon it will be over. I sense an opportunity."

He pounds the pavement in front of the lens, "Which way to the stadium?" He takes a left where he should have gone straight and heads toward Elliot Bay. Another sliver of battery life is gone. I shut off the camera "snap!" and yell down the sidewalk, "Hey you'll end up in the water." He stops, turns around, laughs and bounds back up the hill.

He is sandwiched between gray sky and gray water. Seagulls shadow ferries, skydiving for crusts of bread and muffin bits bought onboard at twice the retail price. A jagged, dirty, green band drapes the horizon. It wavers in the mist like an unsolvable mystery.

"Here's something, maybe we get a shot of me playing my song with the stadium in the background. Hey, why isn't the camera on?"

"The battery is dying. I can't shoot everything."

"Damn, bro, you might miss me doing something great, ha ha ha."

We pass the construction site again, break is over, the beards and suspenders are all back at work, banging it together, plenty of lip whistles, cutting teeth, cutting words, cutting farts, cutting lumber, cutting wire, cutting pipe, cutting tarp, cutting sheetrock, cutting nails, cutting tile, cutting carpet, cutting out.

Somewhere on the Denny Regrade he unzips his backpack, pulls out a Nature Boy power bar and says, "You look terrible, you've got to get into these Nature Boys they're incredible. Did you know the wrapper is biodegradable?"

"I'm just not into power bars. You sure eat a lot of those, what's the calorie count on them anyway?"

"It doesn't matter, BoB's rule number four: Don't be afraid to put on a few extra pounds."

"Really?"

"BoB says no matter how fat you are you can still fly in your dreams. And in this world, famine can strike any minute, a few layers of extra fat can come in handy. Here, try one."

"No thanks."

"No really, here."

"I'm not hungry."

"Stop being like that try it."

"Dude, I don't want your goddamn power bar."

"Alright, no big deal, but you don't know what you're missing, these are a real breakthrough in power bar technology."

I turn on the camera "snap! ding!" and sweep through the background – the buildings, streetlights, all the different lines overhead swinging from pole to pole to building. Who knows what's underground twisting our bowels, stringing us together like some mad umbilical cord fetish.

A few hundred yards from the stadium, he eyeballs an eighteen wheeler blasting Billy Bragg in a parking lot. He makes a beeline for it, hops off the curb, stops four lanes of traffic, jaywalking the street. "Come on, let's go."

The camera says, "That crazy son of a bitch! This ain't no dream mother fucker!"

I follow on a string past all the stalled in the street angry drivers honking, and shouting through their windshields. The camera says, "Hey, swing me around so I can get a look at them and while you're at it, flip them off. Let's see how big a reaction we can get."

He clears the road, crosses the sidewalk, cuts through the parking lot to the side of the rig, sets down his gear, walks up to the truck (a blue Peterbilt "TEAMSTERS LOCAL 206" painted on the side), climbs the passenger side ladder to the cab and pounds on the door. A burly teamster in a blue plaid shirt rolls down the window. He hands him a CD and yells into the Billy Bragg, "Hey man! The Longshoremen are playing my song 'A Bitter Wind is Blowing' it's a protest song I wrote about the WTO."

The burly teamster dials down the Billy Bragg and asks, "What'd you say?"

"I said the Longshoremen are playing my song in the streets, it's on this CD and it's called 'A Bitter Wind is Blowing' you should play it for everyone to hear."

"We only have a cassette deck in here."

"Oh, is there any way to get it on tape?"

"No."

"You guys really need to catch up with technology. You have to hear this it's the right song for the right time. The lyrics are on the inside there, go ahead and give them a read."

The burly teamster smiles and nods his head, he appears stoned out of his gourd to me, smoke is billowing out of the window, he wants to get back to his Billy Bragg, says, "Alright, thanks," and rolls up the window.

He is still clinging to the ladder, but he got a contact high and suddenly he feels light on his feet. He jumps from the third rung. He is heavier than he believes and flatfooted to boot. He plummets to earth, somehow lands on his feet, ankles twist, knees buckle, he falls back on his ass with a "Humph!" straight from the gut. His shell remains intact.

The burly teamster caught it going down, he's clutching his gut he thinks it's so funny. The driver side teamster leans over to get a shot, he spies the aftermath; man down – hilariously, he can hardly take it himself. The burly teamster muffles his laughter and rolls down his window. "Hey, are you alright?"

I intercede, "He's fine," and roll him to his feet.

The camera says, "Humpty Dumpty survives great fall."

We cross Fifth Avenue and close in on the stadium. Sharing the sidewalk with us is a group of union-maids. They are forty to sixty years of age and wearing identical shiny blue nylon jackets covered with union patches.

They're all going at once, like an emancipated henhouse, clucking loud and proud – all cigarettes and liquor. One of them spots the guitar and hoarsely sings, "Someone's got an instrument, hot damn! You gonna play a song?" He cuts in front of her and walks along talking to her over his shoulder. "You may have heard me already. Have you seen the Longshoremen's street blimp?"

"We saw a truck in a parking lot down the street."

"That's the Teamsters' truck, I gave them my CD, they're hoping to get it on tape and give it a play, but really, they need to install a CD player in that thing, I mean, get with the times. They were playing Billy Bragg, can you believe that? He's great and all, but this isn't the eighties, these are more complicated times, more urgent. Anyway, the Longshoremen rented a street blimp for the day and they're playing my song over loudspeakers as they drive through the streets."

"Is that right?"

"Yeah, say, let me give you a copy of my CD."

He pulls one out of his sleeve like a Las Vegas magician, "Voila!" She takes it and stares at the cover; a picture of him standing by some railroad tracks strumming his guitar.

"Ah, sure, I guess, say, we got a little band on the weekends maybe we'll cover it."

"Can you sing? I mean I'm sure you can sing, but this is no ordinary song I put a lot into it."

"Okay, well, thanks."

They continue up the street without us. Goodbye union-maids.

He loves to throw his weight around and talking about his protest song really pumps him up. "I better give her the chord changes and explain the alternate tuning, she'll never figure it out on her own. It's by no means a regular song." He takes off up the sidewalk chasing after the union-maids.

The battery is down yet another sliver. I shoot the world cockeyed as I limp toward the stadium. Pain in my chest, eyes bleeding a gooey white substance, my goddamn gimpy knee is acting up. I can't see anything in the shadow of the Space Needle.

I catch up with him near the stadium entrance, finishing off a Nature Boy. He looks well rested. The stands loom overhead. I've about had it. "Goddamn it, this just seems like a waste of time."

"It'll be worth the effort, just you wait and see. This is a call of duty – stuff they need to know."

"Don't you think they already know? They're here for Christ's sake."

"This is important stuff and they're walking around dressed as sea turtles or whatever, and dancing! They're missing a golden opportunity! How can they dance when the world is about to end?"

There is a steady flow of people heading toward the entrance and he tries to engage them all; handing out CDs and Nature Boy power bars to the willing.

He follows a little girl carrying a hand-crayoned protest sign. She's with her mother. He steps on her heels, "Hey, you in the blue coat, can I ask you about your sign? So, the WTO is taking away our laws? Huh? I suppose that's true in a way, but let me give your mom my CD. Don't worry, it's kid friendly."

We bob up and down in a stagnant sea of people at the entrance. Someone is yelling, "Sign-in to be counted!" Someone else, "Free rain ponchos!" He takes two clear plastic ponchos, slides to the side and slips one of them over his cardboard amplifier. "That'll do the trick."

From under the bleachers we hear a female voice over the loudspeakers. "Sisters and brothers, we are the story of the WTO and the WTO will never be the same!" The crowd cheers.

We enter the stadium and climb into the bleachers. It's a party. There are giant puppets, signs galore, every way possible to say "No WTO".

The crowd on the field stand in patches of yellow, purple, blue and red slickers, there are various gray white tents. "The people united can never be defeated."

In the stands next to the scoreboard there is a giant inflated rat with red eyes and a sign around its neck "Fair trade is not free trade."

On stage, a plump Latina in blue is at the microphone giving it all she's got.

Stage right, a woman is signing for the deaf. At the rear of the stage there is a small lineup of speakers-to-come.

The plump Latina is the one we heard from under the bleachers. The audience loves her. She tells it like it is outside in the broad daylight.

The sun peeks through and a rainbow appears over the stadium, but is eventually snuffed out by the clouds. Fair is fair is fair.

"There's got to be sixty thousand people here. It's great, but you know what the media will do, they'll say there's only thirty and there certainly won't be any sound-bites from this lady. Let's get back to Fourth. This is going to break up soon, I can feel it, if we leave now we'll get ahead of the pack and be setup and waiting. You'll want to save some battery for that."

Just outside the stadium we pass a row of porta potties butted against a wall. Doors spring open and slam shut as the protesters enter and exit. The piss and shit are flowing, doused in chemicals, soon to be heading somewhere else, out of sight out of mind. Perhaps it would be better if everyone just shit right in the street for a day so we can get a true accounting of the mess we're making.

Past the porta potties – in the mix of vertical stripes angling the concrete square – there is a large man in blue jeans, a blue shirt, a black trench coat, a cowboy hat. He's covered with buttons. He's handing out leaflets and pleading his case to anyone who will listen. "I'm a steel worker and I've been locked out of Kaiser Aluminum for fifteen months."

I try to zoom-in on his buttons, but they blur in the viewfinder. Another sliver of battery life is gone. I kick myself on the concrete square muttering through clenched teeth, "Why didn't I spring for another battery? Cheapskate sonofabitch." The camera says, "I hear that, one lousy five hour battery for a ten hour day, brilliant planning dipshit. You should know by now; whatever I don't get on tape is subject to endless speculation."

We head toward Fifth. There's a loudspeaker blaring in the street, "Come on the Rising Wind" by Creedence Clearwater Revival.

On a corner we run into a group of topless women with black electrical tape over their nipples, yellow plastic "CAUTION" tape around their necks and waists and arms and ears and legs.

They are "BGH Free" it's scrawled over their naked torsos in black magic marker and paint. It looks as though they threw the idea together this morning. Likely, it's the last in a line of inspirations that began with dressing up like ballerinas and echoing spoken word through megaphones. Who can blame them? There is something in the air, an orbiting chaos, a peace loving freak festival bursting with mediocre creativity.

These are the college educated, everybody-is-an-artist-in-their-own-way, class of the higher conscience than you. He stands above them all, mugging for the camera, a rounder Benny Hill.

He approaches the nearest BGH-Free woman and asks, "So you're BGH free, but do you really understand the Bovine Growth Hormone issues?"

She doesn't quite know what to say, she stares at him with a are-you-kidding-me? look on her face as he proceeds to give her a lesson on the ups and downs, ins and outs of BGH. She shakes her head continually, yes, yes, yes, she already knows all that. He pushes forward as she pulls away. The frame is not wide enough for the both of them. She breaks out and poses in another direction.

Arriving on the scene; a group of girls and boys dressed as superheroes. They smash into the BGH-Free women, chanting, "There ain't no power like the power of the people 'cause the power of the people don't stop." They dance, twirl, do the bump and grind.

There's a posse of dreds across the street beating on drums, pots, pans, street signs, asphalt, glass, brickwork. Suddenly there's another cloudburst and a rush of wind from across the water. It sends the yellow "CAUTION" tape flying, slapping thighs and spanking bottoms. All the black electrical tape is stripped off and blown into the street. Nobody runs for cover. The BGH-Free women with their glistening nipples, pink and pointing, hold their own. Forty-two degrees or there about and they are steaming.

The group of super heroes veers off and dances on down the street – they only dealt a glancing blow. Still, he is dizzy, his stomach is growling, he needs another power bar, he can't remember why he came here in the first place, has no idea which way to go either. He taps his toes to the dreds' wicked beat and hugs his clear plastic poncho-wrapped cardboard amp like a teddy bear (I half expect him to start sucking his thumb). The tip of the mic stand teeters above the fray like Vlad's pike awaiting its severed head.

The camera asks, "Why aren't we recording this? This is priceless."

"I thought we were recording. Goddamn it!" I hit record (the same button alternates between pause and record) as he bolts down the sidewalk putting the beating drums and the BGH-Free women far behind.

I follow slowly and at a distance, cursing myself for missing all that good action, nothing now, but the back of his head bobbing through a crosswalk and on top of that he's heading in the wrong direction.

I don't have the desire to keep him on course. There are no straight lines in this goddamn city. He may be one hundred yards ahead, but certainly he's running out of gas, there must be an oxygen shortage in his blood, surely his lungs are heaving like an old accordion; one you might find in an attic full of dust and rat shit.

He returns to the front of the camera, fully restored by the miracle of Nature Boy power bars, "Mmm mm these are good. You know, the problem with the topless lesbians is that they are the ones who are going to get on the news and people will be like, what a bunch of weirdoes, and there goes the movement. I was thinking of telling them that as a matter of fact I should have. One should speak one's mind these days."

We paddle down Fifth passing the EMP museum, construction abounds, plenty of plywood shelling the sidewalk – obscuring the view of a rich guy's cow pie.

A bale of sea turtles waddle past and he throws a net, "Hey, the news said you are protesting the environment, how about that?"

They laugh sarcastically, mothers with children, little sea turtles tagging along. "Yeah, we're *against* the environment. Leave it to the media."

He tries to hold them in the net, they snap through his web with their sharp beaks and continue up the street without him.

He says to the camera, "I wanted to give those sea turtles a copy of my CD, but they were in such a hurry, can you believe it? Sea turtles in a hurry."

He bursts into song right there in the cold damp street; the Creedence Clearwater Revival song we heard earlier:

> "Come on a risin'
> wind, we're
>
> goin' up around
> the bend, do, do,
>
> do, do, do, do, do,
> do, do."

The camera says, "I don't see the point in all this. Does this guy really believe he's worthy of a classic and to be singing it wrong and off key?"

I laugh and my head pounds and pounds, my goddamn eyeball is glued to the lens. The world is wider than it is tall.

Holding up the monorail are gray concrete pylons decorated with "No WTO" in black spray paint. Twice, I've run into them with blunt toes; pain rolling like a wave up my spine and breaking over the sand in my head.

Most of the businesses we pass are shuttered. Nothing but vacant squares, nervous security, skeptical neighbors and polite, part-time parking lot attendants – everyone else is protest related.

The slickers and backpacks stroll past us in groups of five, ten, twenty, forty, sixty, three hundred. We are going against the flow. He tries to turn them around with, "If you're heading to the stadium, it's packed to the upper rows, no use going that way when they'll soon be coming this way, follow me, I've got a song to sing."

Nobody answers his call. They're already making music with whistles and sirens and slogans and shakers and air horns and plastic drums.

In a fake southern drawl, the camera mocks, "That mother fucker thinks he's the pied piper."

We turn down Bell Street, cross Fourth Avenue, then Third. He stops on the sidewalk, sets down his gear, tilts his head, cocks an ear. "Listen, hear those drums? I've heard them before in San Francisco. I don't remember the cause we were fighting for, but that beat is the same used by a group of anarchists who like to tear things up."

"I can't picture anarchists beating on drums."

"Believe it! That's what I thought at the time, but those buggers kicked over my amp and hollered 'Anarchy!' into my microphone. I don't advocate that kind of behavior. BoB's rule number three: Don't placate the bastards."

On the next block, the sidewalk is clogged with scaffolding – just another Belltown high-rise reaching into oblivion.

We're overtaken by a large group of demonstrators; a motley, independent crew. He's surprised and mortified. "What're they doing on Third?" They takeover the street. We are sucked into their wake.

Everyone is over the top and out of control. We're in this together right? We blend with the trucks and vans, the energy is fantastic – the sewers are burning, the manholes are bleeding – it radiates off our great mass and rises up into the gray overcast. We won't see the sun again in our lifetimes, we'll make our own heat, we'll rub sticks together, there are plenty holding up the protest signs, after that, who knows?

Third Avenue is full of runoff from the protest: the roughnecks, the painted-ons and the worn-throughs. There are enough instrumentalists on the street, more or less working together, to send him scurrying to Second Avenue then First where he hooks south and zigzags between First and Third eventually running into the Indy media outlet.

We step through the storefront. There is a crowd here too. Fifteen PCs line the walls with fifteen hunchbacks a tap, tap, tapping, fifteen bend-overs keeping tabs and fifteen more settling scores.

It is a newsroom, bunkhouse and recreation center led by some brother Smith with too much confidence.

He plants himself in front of the brother Smith and offers to sing his song as a morale booster, "Looks like you guys could use a pick-me-up. How about I play my song for everyone? It's the right song for the right time."

The brother Smith barely gives him a glance, "There isn't a minute to spare. Don't you see this is unprecedented? We're getting it in real-time, broadcasting on the internet, taking the media back, breaking the paradigm. The news will never be the same and we are leading the charge."

I push him out of there and back onto the sidewalk. "If we stay here too long they'll put us to work."

"Yeah, you're right, let's get back to Fourth. Now the vibe is right."

□

We head north on Third then cut to Fourth on Lenora Street. We pick up the roar of a crowd off in the distance, south toward Westlake – we overshot. The roar subsides, an exuberant voice fills the gap (aided by fifty watt speakers) with a rat-ta-tat verse.

The crowd bellows its chorus on cue and in perfect measures. From here, there are no words, everything is washed out, it's just a lot of heavy breathing. "I think we missed the march from the stadium. Sounds like everyone is already at Westlake."

"That can't be true, there must be more coming. My gut is telling me to stick to Fourth. I'm sure we can find a good awning to play under."

The crowd breaks into another chorus. The camera says, "Listen to that shit. Don't they know they can't isolate the truth? Everything turns to mush. The only thing that matters is what is happening right now in front of the fucking lens."

Coming down the sidewalk is an eight foot tall city worker, a garbage collector, a human street sweeper, pushing a gray plastic garbage can bungee strapped to a dolly (hand-truck).

There is a broom with a cracked shaft, reinforced with duct tape, jammed between the dolly and garbage can along with a dust pan and extra garbage bags.

He's dressed in bright yellow rain gear. A two piece number with a hood cinched tight over a baseball cap that reads 'Ballard Plumbing' in faded red stitching and grease stains. He has a tiny, blue safety vest cinched tight around his middle squeezing him like a twice used tube of toothpaste.

He hardly needs the safety vest, it's a mere spot of blue on a yellow sequoia.

He is stiff from the neck down; like his spine has fused together in two or three different places. He compensates with exceptional knees that do all the lifting.

His head is a wobbly lighthouse riding the low clouds that push down from the sky only seven feet off the ground. He is beaming the street with his rheumy blue eyes.

He cannot bend forward or lean back so remains straight as an arrow as he pushes the dolly with one hand while the other squeezes the handle of a long plastic stick that looks permanently attached at the wrist – a full blown extension of his greater self. It's a device he uses, in conjunction with his tremendous knees, to bend and pluck the garbage off the street then rise up and flick it into the can.

He swings the pickup stick like an electric guitar. He is all wah wah and whammy, does midair splits (ala Pete Townsend) with a stiff upper back and lip, snatching riffs right out of the air: blowing leaves, hamburger wrappers, little birdies, rubber bullets.

He knocks the city worker out of his zen jam with, "So, it's pretty messy today, huh?" The city worker stops, sticks out his lower lip, catches his breath, spots a cigarette butt stuck in a concrete crack, squats down on his herculean knees and tries to pinch it with the pickup stick. "Aah, well, I was…

because it's not… I thought your parade was gonna be a little bit bigger… has the parade started yet?"

"No way, no how, there are at least sixty thousand that will be marching down here from the stadium."

"Oh, hey, ah, guys, does the parade go down Fifth and up Fourth?" He continues to pluck at the cigarette butt with his pick-up stick.

"No, down Fourth then up Fifth."

"Okay, I'll be well out of your way by tomorrow." Suddenly he's aware of the camera cutting him off at the neck. He looks into the lens and says, "Well, thank you," and laughs uncomfortably. I back off as he gives his own direction, "Oh, ah, smile, wave," he smiles, waves a giant yellow hand then goes back to the cigarette butt in the crack. "Ah, tomorrow morning I'll be very busy. I'll probably be out here very early. You know, all the guys, the protesters and whatnot, they're all, aah, they're really neat ya know. They come up to the bucket and ask 'May I?' Well sure you can, you can use the bucket."

"Yeah, these people care. So, do you like your job? I'll bet you expend a lot of energy on the job, huh?"

"Yeah, I do, but, ya know, they're always tryin' to improve things for us down here. Like this thing here," he shakes his pick-up stick, "I use to pick up the refuse. They said that they were trying to prevent back injuries, ya know, from all the bending over, ya see, which was costing them a lot in disability expenses what with the insurance that covers it and whatnot. Something like that. But now with these things we all have carpal tunnel from squeezing them all day and our insurance doesn't cover it so we're stuck, worse off than before. I gotta tell ya if I wasn't working today I'd be right with you guys." He squats lower and bevels into the crack with the end of his pick-up stick and nudges the cigarette butt toward a shallow end.

"Cool."

"I'm sure there's gonna be some changes, I really do, but a lot of people who talk to me are afraid this is gonna turn into a Chicago thing, ya know, back in the sixties, and I say 'No, these are good people, these people from the other side.'" He nips the cigarette butt, rises to his full eight feet and flips the butt into the can.

"These are people from across the entire spectrum of society. They're all here. After today the media will have no choice but to hear our voices."

The city worker has to get moving, he's on the clock, there's a mess back where we came from. He remains hopeful, "Ah, well, good luck to all," then he tilts back the dolly and pushes it down the street, snapping a Nature Boy power bar wrapper off the sidewalk.

"Did you hear him call it a parade? A parade! The way the media broadcasts all those damn puppets and belly dancers it's no wonder the guy on the street thinks it's a parade. This is serous business. This movement could use an articulate voice. We've got to get me in front of a news camera. Let's keep our eyes open for one of the networks or CNN."

We bump into Denny Way again. I didn't even know we were moving north. I'm all turned around – slabbing the outskirts – which way? I don't know.

We see a march in progress. "I'm going to run over and see what's up."

I catch the protesters at the Five Point where they angle off Denny and back onto Fifth. The march has run up against the mass of demonstrators who arrived earlier. They're trying to push themselves into Westlake Center, but it's still eight blocks away. The camera says, "This turkey is stuffed."

A series of polite cheers from the demonstrators ripple down the monorail line. Everyone is dutifully assembling. The camera says, "This fucking thing is Mardi Gras, Cinco de Mayo, a renaissance fair, a Grateful Dead show, a PTA meeting, and a plumbers convention all rolled into one."

"Yeah, well, they're passionate."

"Passionate? Can't you see what I'm getting on tape?"

Everything is at a standstill. The crowd has pushed in upon itself, it could be a compressed spring or that gassed-out old accordion filled with dust and rat shit. A collective groan rises from the collective belly. There is hardly enough air left to squeeze out a decent chant. All quiet on the liberal front.

There is no beginning or end. This is the muddy middle where the current swirls. Small parties collide in the frame and exit slightly altered. Here, the illusion is strongest; where everyone believes they are following their own path as they twirl in blooming whirlpools being pushed down a mighty river.

I point the camera down the street (opposite the crowd) a Nature Boy power bar wrapper rolls through the frame like a tumbleweed. Further down and out of focus, his egg shell enters a convenience store. The camera complains, "That guy has no fucking limits."

"At least his heart is in the right place."

"Yes, the devastation wrought by good hearts. You assholes should study your own history."

"What the hell are you talking about?"

"Exactly."

I shut down the camera, "snap!" hustle down the street toward the convenience store, step inside and find him near the cooler. "Looks like the march from the stadium is going down Fifth. They're really hammered in there. It's the perfect place to play."

"Then we'll catch them when they loop around on Fourth."

"What if they don't loop around?"

"It's perfectly logical that they will. Do you want anything to drink?"

"No, I'm good."

"You sure? I'll get you something."

"Really, I'm fine."

"It's not a problem."

"Thanks, but I'm good."

"Suit yourself."

He opts for a Snapple, beef jerky and an apple fritter then steps to the counter and says to the cashier, "You should stock Nature Boy power bars. You would make a fortune. I'll bet no one else in town has them, you could be the first." He pulls one from his backpack and holds it up, "You've got to try this. I know you're going to love it." He turns it over. "There's contact information on the back of the wrapper if you want to order some for your store. I'll leave this sample with you."

"I'll give it to the boss."

"Thanks man and here's another one for you, nothing like an employee testimonial to get the ball rolling."

The cashier sets them aside and rings him up. "That'll be eight sixty-five."

He searches his pockets, turns to the camera, "Do you have a couple bucks?"

I pull out a ten. "This is all I have."

"Thanks." He takes the ten and turns back to the cashier, "Man you gotta try that Nature Boy, you really do, here, let me show you how easy it is to unwrap." He reaches across the counter for one of the power bars, "Look here, either end will do, you just tear it off, see, both ends are perforated." He rips it open and shoves it in front of the cashier. "Here, take a bite, you'll absolutely love it." The cashier is frowning (has been frowning the entire time) he looks like he isn't having a good day maybe not a bad day, but certainly not a good one. He grips the Nature Boy, takes a bite and chews silently. "Well, what do you think?" The cashier shrugs his shoulders, still frowning, "It's alright."

"Alright? Are you telling me that's not the best power bar you have ever tasted?"

"They all taste pretty much the same to me."

"Whatever." He hands the cashier my money. "I just don't understand how you can believe that they all taste alike."

I turn-on the camera and wander over to a window where an ice box filled with last summer's frozen treats (now buried in a thick layer of frost) is pushed up against the windowsill. The camera says, "Set me down and point me through the glass. I'll get a shot of the street."

It's a nice angle, people on the move, unaware of the lens, pouring over the hill, obeying the traffic signs, blinking lights, power lines, bare trees, naked bums, fake jewelry, seagulls, sirens, ringing doorways, loose transactions, salt and pepper spray.

□

Heading south on Fourth toward Westlake Center we pass the same construction site for the third time. It seems we have stomped on nearly every square inch of Denny Regrade, lower Queen Anne and Belltown – twice maybe three times and we haven't gotten anywhere.

The street is empty for the most part. All the action is on Fifth. The few straggling protesters in the concrete canal are like a trickle from a dam as they head away from downtown. I could be one of them; the early leavers, muttering to themselves, I'm surprised I stayed this long, as they trickle up the street.

He is barely moving down the sidewalk. He is finally feeling the weight of his disposition, "Dammit, why am I doing this? I figured there'd be more protesters here. Where did everyone go? It's perfectly logical that if they're going down Fifth, they'll be coming up Fourth. I'll bet the cops are redirecting the march and nobody knows what's going on. We need to get to the bottom of this."

Raindrops are falling again; nice fat ones. Ten degrees cooler and they'd be mighty hailstones pulverizing the scene. He spots an awning, limps out of the rain and drops his load by a door. "This will do if the damn march would just show up." He pulls out a Nature Boy, rips at the perforation and squeezes from the bottom pushing the turdish looking power bar out like a brown Otter Pop. He sinks his teeth in, chews slowly, sighs, "Man, that apple fritter about did me in. But I'm feeling better now. Good thing I've got these Nature Boys huh? When are you going to try one?"

"Never."

The rain backs off and the sun pops through the clouds but then the clouds fill the hole and we stoop a little lower.

We are saturated. The surface is ninety-five percent liquid, it's not a stretch to say we are all wet. But it's the best we can expect for a late autumn day in the Pacific Northwest.

He turns from gazing at the street to staring through a plate-glass window that is situated under the awning. "Hey, I think that's a radio station in there. I wonder if they play music?" The glass is tinted. I can't see anything.

A woman wearing a dark blue skirt-suit and low pumps, blond hair in a bob-cut, exits the building. He steps in front of her, clears his throat and points at the plate-glass, "Excuse me, can you tell me if that's a radio station in there?"

She arcs around his midsection like a tiny moon circling Jupiter. She clears his massive rump, spots the camera rising above the horizon, wrinkles her nose, squints hard at the lens, takes herself out of orbit with two lunar steps down the sidewalk then rotates on her axis. "Ah, I have no idea. I usually don't come down this side of the building."

He tries to slow her escape, "Oh. So you must have a good view of the protest?"

She takes two more lunar steps down the sidewalk, shakes her blond bob-cut, "Oh, I don't live here, I mean, I live in Seattle, but not here."

His pull is weak despite his great mass, "So what do you think about the protest?"

"I'm not interested in the WTO at all." She furrows her brow, takes another lunar step down the sidewalk.

"You're not interested?"

"Nope, not at all." She bounds out of sight.

He is astonished, flabbergasted, just plain put out. "She's not interested. That takes an amazing amount of disinterest. That takes like, willful disinterest. This is the biggest story of the decade and she's not interested. I should have said that to her, dammit! Problem is I'm too slow on the upswing."

He steps into the street, shades his eyes with a hand over his brow and gazes up the wet asphalt. I swing the camera around and catch a tiny group of one, three, five, seven brass monkeys: tubas, trombones and trumpets playing two, four, six different tunes.

Following close behind the brass monkeys are a ten foot tall pirate shaking a giant baby rattle, a dude carrying the planet in a cage and a guy on snare. Nothing out of the ordinary today. The camera says, "Somebody's garage sure must be a fucking mess."

Coming the opposite direction are twenty-seven mothers-to-be carrying identical green and white striped umbrellas, chanting, "What do we want? Diversity! When do we want it? Now!"

Five of the mothers-to-be grip a large banner with five swollen hands "No Patents on Life" get out of the way they're moving fast right down the middle of the street.

He attempts to cross in front of them. They sweep him along with their banner and pop him out near Blanchard Street. The camera says, "Look, they gave birth to a three hundred fifty pound baby protest singer; talk about your labor pains."

He makes his way back down the sidewalk, all pink and pouting and sucking on a Nature Boy power bar. "Did you see that? Those ladies wouldn't let up for a second. I hope you didn't get that on tape."

I did.

The rain subsides. He stays put under the awning. A man wearing coke bottle glasses – and press credentials strung around his neck – crosses the frame. "So, who are you press with?"

The man slows, swivels his head toward the camera, blinks twice behind his large round magnified lenses, "Huh?"

He grabs his arm and spins him around. "Who are you press with?"

The man pirouettes, breaks free from his grasp, backtracks, "Oh, the Stranger."

He is swept to one knee, a last chunk of power bar squeezes down his throat, "Yeah?"

The man gives a slight bow to the camera, "Yeah, always," and retreats down the street.

A guy and girl wearing matching windbreakers walk through the lens.

He gets between them with, "Hey, I have a question for you guys."

They pause for a second, eyeball the camera, look annoyed – they don't like being wedged apart – reluctantly, the guy asks, "What is it?"

"Well, when I'm talking to people on the street about the WTO their response is usually 'Why don't you just vote?' When you tell people about the issues and that's their response, what do you say?"

The guy answers as the girl tugs on his arm as if to pull him offstage – he is giving up ground in inches. "We don't talk to people that way, we're not trying to convert anyone, if they want to come down here and join in, that's cool."

She drags him out of the lens. They walk away in unison.

He watches until they're out of sight then turns to the camera and laughs and laughs. "They're not trying to convert anyone. Can you believe that?"

The roar of ten thousand house cats erupts in the street, from the north, I think. The camera asks, "What the hell is that?" I pan through the background looking for an open sore, but all I find is a riot cop with a walrus mustache, strutting toward us on the sidewalk. The camera says, "Jesus fucking Christ! He'll eat all the fish in the harbor."

The riot cop bears down on the lens swinging his arms loose and free, his head pivoting side to side, scanning two hundred forty degrees – a great parabolic arc.

"Can I ask you a question?"

The riot cop shortens his strut, "Sure."

"Aside from the protesters and all that what is your opinion of the WTO?"

"I can't express my opinion while in uniform, but I will say that there are many who are sympathetic to the cause." He struts south toward some unknown position.

An organic trio arrives on the scene: two thin beards and an anemic girl. They are hemp down to their underwear. Each one is carrying a cardboard cutout colored with nontoxic paint and wired to tree branches gathered from Volunteer Park. They swear by their medicine cards. They know their totem animals. This morning two out of three pulled the buffalo card: abundance. This will be a good day of togetherness and humility. Give thanks for all will be provided.

He jerks them to the side, "Hey you guys let me ask you a question." They notice the camera, one thin beard stands front and center, one thin beard leans on the edge of the frame, the anemic girl plugs the background. "When you're in the street do you try to engage people from the other side maybe teach them the truth about the WTO?"

"We are about compassion and understanding. We're not interested in preaching to people. They have their side and we respect that."

Already there is tension in the group, the other thin beard wants out of the scene, the anemic girl is sympathetic, but the thin beard standing front and center holds them in place.

"Well how are we going to get through to them without at least engaging them in conversation? The media is keeping them dumb and in the dark."

"I agree, I've heard some misinformation out there, but I don't want to have a negative interaction by opening a can of worms, you know what I mean? So, I agree with you up to that point."

"But why? There's a whole line of thought out there that's based on ignorance. How do you get through?" I frame his frown in profile against a damp brick building.

"Live by example."

"Man, that's not going to work. I've been studying these issues for nearly six months. I read everything I can get my hands on. I talk to everybody, bus drivers, you name it. We've got to get through to people, it doesn't matter if they're for the cause if they don't know why they're for the cause."

"To each his own, I guess."

"Oh, by the way, here's a copy of my CD." He pulls it from a back pocket and forces it on the thin beard.

The thin beard says, "Thanks, well, good luck," and turns to find that his friends are gone. They slipped away without anyone noticing. Even the camera is at a loss, "I swear, they were here a second ago."

There is a two hundred piece mariachi band drunk on tequila coming our way. They are playing at different tempos and in different keys. The trumpets are all over the place, the violins are down to two strings precariously balanced. It is a brightly colored affair in the middle of the doom and gloom downtown.

This just might be the front end of the long awaited parade. The street sweeper was right he'll be out here early tomorrow. Cleaning up a beautiful mess. The camera says, "We need to walk along in the center of that and shoot from there. Backwards, forwards, side to side, it's all good."

"You don't want to see me on tequila."

"It can't be worse than this."

He steps in front of the camera and blots out the parade. "Man that's terrible, there's no way I can play over the top of that. Let's go."

The camera is incensed. "Every time there is something interesting going on that fucking toad hops away. I don't get it."

We pass the Bon Marche'; one of those block long and block wide city department stores that operates like a casino. One hundred percent artificial lighting and under lock and key. The doorman is letting in the regulars one at a time then locking the door afterward.

It's a solemn day, serious, grim. The employees stand behind the window displays stiff like the mannequins, chewing their nails, powdering their noses, drenched in christmas red.

At the makeup counter an emaciated forty year veteran saleswoman discusses the crisis with an emaciated rookie salesgirl who asks, "What should we do if they break windows and start looting?"

"We are not to prevent them from looting. That would be imprudent anyway. Stick with me and don't worry my dear we will get away the safest way possible."

Mid-block in front of the Bon Marche' display windows, he stops and begins to set up his equipment. He pulls the microphone (already attached to the cord) from his backpack and strings it to the amp. He does the same with the guitar then clicks on the amp and fiddles the knobs.

He has set up at least a couple hundred feet from the mass of demonstrators still cramming the center from Fifth. I drop the lens and ask, "What are you doing? The crowd's over there."

"You gotta give them some space to come forward and gather around. The key is to be within earshot and creating a scene. They'll fill the space."

He straps on the guitar, puts his mouth to the mic, "Check, check, one, two, three," strums the guitar, adjusts the volume and tone. He spends an inordinate amount of time making minute adjustments to the amp and guitar then says to the mostly empty street, "Okay, this is a protest song, stuff you should all know, you should all be talking about with people because most people have no idea what's going on." He jangles an intro on his guitar then sings, "This is it – my people – we're in for it – my people – the government – is evil – there's gonna be an – upheaval – a bitter wind is blowing – a bitter wind is blowing."

He's a jitterbug Dylan

"It's just free trade they say but it ain't all that. It ain't freeeee – if you can't seeeeee – what's beneeeeeath. Yeah! a bitter wind is blowing – a bitter wind is blowing – a bitter wind is blowing – a bitter wind is blowing – a bitter wind is bloooooooowwwwwing..."

A crowd doesn't form in front of the cardboard amp. Even the mannequins in the display windows are looking away. The small groups of protesters who pass drop their heads and quicken their pace or veer off when they see the camera. I don't blame them. I would orbit the moon to avoid the front of the lens.

The few who pause at the outer ring scrunch their faces, gaze at the camera, turn to the scrunched face next to them and ask, "What is this about?"

"Who knows?"

"Is everything worth videotaping?"

"Good question."

Then they step away, but can't help a backward glance, these contentious objectors give it their best trying to understand, "He's quite literal isn't he?" only to be replaced by two or three more who do and say much the same.

It is harder and harder to keep him in the frame. The camera is fighting me and it's making his egg curve difficult to focus; he's just a giant blur. Another sliver of battery disappears then another in quick succession. My headache is puking pain and gravy. The camera demands, "You better point me somewhere else or I'll bleed this fucking battery dry and then where will you be? I'll shred my built-in microphone. I'd rather kill myself than have to look at this."

"Listen, I'm having my own problems here, I'm nearsighted as it is and squinting through your tiny eyehole is not working for me. I'm going to use the flip-out screen."

"Are you fucking nuts! You'll burn out the battery in half the time."

"So be it."

The camera snorts, coughs, gags, jolts, squeals. There is a cracking sound then a clean snap. Suddenly it's out of breath. It whispers something hard to make out, something tinny, trebly, way down in its whirling drive, its grinding gears.

I pull the camera up, tilt my head and lean in with my good ear. The one that hasn't yet succumbed to this screeching world. The camera laughs weakly and says, "I broke the latch from the inside, mother fucker. I can't let you jeopardize the mission because you have a little headache. Now you listen to me, pan left and frame that crowd in the distance. Hear that bellowing? See that bursting cumulus? That just might be tear gas blowing out of the alleys. The buildings are swaying, see that shaking glass? Foundations are rumbling, soon they may be on fire, go, go, go, frame it up, frame it up."

"You goddamn piece of shit I should throw you in the garbage."

"Chill the fuck out, the latch is a cheap fix. The question is where do we go from here?"

"I made a commitment to see this through to the end. This was my idea. I can't bale on him now."

"Listen, do you want to get to the truth of it or shoot a pointless story about a wandering asshole? Come on, let's leave this chump behind, something stinks, he's probably got a stake in those fucking power bars the way he's pitching them around. It feels like we're shooting a commercial. The nerve of some people, huh? What're we doing?"

I put him in the frame once more, he is really going at it this protest singer, flailing away at the guitar, his outer rim undulating with every adamant tap of his foot. The lyrics are falling out of his mouth and landing on the sidewalk in front of him; piling up like black plastic garbage bags during a garbage strike. His ambition, his resolve, his tenacity, his fortitude, his Nature Boy power bars, are contained therein.

A siren voice is coming through a PA way off somewhere and she's getting rousing applause from the crowd. I try to pull her in with a long zoom, but I can't find her, there's no telling which direction she is in. Her voice is bouncing off the buildings. The camera says, "Now that's worth looking for."

☐

"They must not be able to hear me from over there. Man, I should have brought a bigger amp."

He packs up and edges his way to the edge of the protest, sniffs the air; the corner of Fourth Avenue and Pine Street across from Westlake Center. The people are unusually sedate. "This is perfect." He sets up and again spends an excruciating amount of time fine-tuning his instrument. The camera says, "Jesus H Christ, this isn't Carnegie Hall, jackass."

Eventually he dives into his tune. The crowd scatters. The camera says, "Here's our chance, he'll be blowing that bitter wind for twenty minutes at least, let's hit it."

I weave through the street, quick framing the demonstrators. I don't give them time to blink, to bow out of the way, to breathe.

A chanting crowd of a couple thousand marches toward the lens. Different colors and slogans melt together, pull apart, some take rights, some take lefts, some sink into the pavement. The camera is breathing easier here.

Two men settle next to the lens as the marchers pass and despite the roar of the crowd they come through clear enough.

One of them is a newspaper vendor; a big mustache of a man with a cigarette hanging slack from a mouth with few teeth. He's wearing a dark smock "Seattle Times" printed on the front.

The other one is shorter, younger and zipped up in a gray hoodie. He looks like a young Charles Manson; shaggy, intense, a little cross-eyed. He says to the big mustache, "I seen a national guard unit down here today!"

The big mustache pushes it aside with a rasp, "Ahhh, they don't need it."

The gray hoodie is emphatic, "The anarchists are breaking windows and shit!"

The big mustache waves him away and hacks, "That's nothing."

The gray hoodie counters, "Yeah, but then that spurs the fucking cops to throw tear gas and shoot rubber bullets."

The big mustache cuts him down, coughs, "They were going to do that anyway." He extends an arm toward the street, "These people didn't come down here to break windows. They just wanted to make a point. Even if they're just standing there, when the cops want the intersection, they take the intersection."

"Yeah, well, I don't want to get caught in a roundup and carted off to jail. I got shit pending."

"You from around here?"

"Nah, I'm from L.A."

I head back to the corner where he is still jangling his protest song. Someone shouts, "Play Free Bird!" That causes a couple others to whoop-it-up, soon everyone is knocking against his looping chorus, "A bitter wind is blowing – a bitter wind is blowing," with loud whistles and a "Hey!" "Yeah!" "Fuck!"

He proves stronger than the crowd, he pitches it into the light drizzle, "A bitter wind is blowing – a bitter wind is blowing." I center him in the frame "a bitter wind is blowing – a bitter wind is blowing..."

He is all worked up and feeding off the crowd's hostility. He is picking up speed and volume like louder and faster are the keys. Suddenly, the gray hoodie steps into the frame, grabs the microphone, pushes him aside and peppers the grill, "The WTO conference has been shutdown. They ended up with only two hundred delegates. About twenty minutes ago I heard from a news reporter that the conference is shutdown for the day because they can't gather. The streets are too crowded. They can't make their meetings."

The crowd closes in – shouting, clapping, whistling – as the gray hoodie steps away from the microphone. I follow him with the camera as he turns and walks up the street, stops, turns back and yells, "That's for today, we got another day tomorrow!" Somebody screams, "Yeah, baby, yeah!" There's some spotted laughter, sniffing and sneezing. The gray hoodie disappears into the mob.

I swing the camera back to the mic just as he kicks back into the song exactly where he was pushed aside. Now he is really annoyed, he puts it all in the performance. The people scatter before he hits the chorus.

I wander away again looking for some action. I shoot a woman through a window. She is lost in her thoughts as she pecks at a salad. She stares straight ahead, not blinking, there's no street out there, it's all just chicken feed.

Two stools to her right there is a man chomping on a tortilla wrap. He seems just as bored, he's like a cow in a barn chewing its cud.

At this end of the protest the groups are smaller; five to ten slickers backpacked together in semi-circles or strung out along the street and sidewalk. What to do next is the general topic, that and, where are the rest of the group?

There are a few milling around in business suits, drinking lattes and smirking at the goings-on.

This is an afternoon adventure for others. Something they needed to see for themselves. They squawk into their cell phones, "Yeah, I'm down by Westlake, what a mess!"

I step along the sidewalk and run the camera lens up and down the buildings, twirl and somer-sault. I get a shot through four layers of glass. All the movement from the street is fractured and reflecting on the panes. It's one truly fucked up collage. This will represent the chaos in the streets, brilliant! The camera says, "Knock it off with that bullshit."

A large splinter group comes marching up Pine Street. A man with a megaphone is leading the charge while an old woman in a yellow slicker clutches his arm and struggles along next to him as he yells into the megaphone. It is difficult to pick up what he is saying. "We are the people of the third tier. We are here from all over the world: Vietnam, Malaysia, Thailand…"

A thin line of blood red slickers follows the megaphone. The march is thick with signs, flags, banners, paint bucket drums, masked protesters, single cell demonstrators, a coalition of causes: "Trade With Cuba" "League of Filipino Workers" "People's Conference Against Imperialists Globalization" "People Before Profits" "Junk APEC!" "WTO Sucks!"

A dishpan band brings up the rear. The march is absorbed by the Westlake mob where more megaphones bark at the crowd, "Hell no WTO, Hell no WTO."

"Who's got the power?"

"We've got the power!"

"Who's got the power?"

"We've got the power!"

"Power to the people!"

He resolves to an E minor, sheds the guitar, sets it in its case and shuts down the cardboard amp. "There's always someone in the crowd who wants the microphone. I broke BoB's rule number two: Never relinquish control. One time I was playing and some homeless guy interrupted me, saying, 'I want to read a poem I wrote.' Well, I'm like, 'are you any good?' I can't hand over the microphone to just anybody. Anyway, he was at the mic for over a half hour! Come on, if you can't edit your poem down to at least five minutes, chances are it sucks. But hey, we shutdown the WTO today how cool is that?"

A street blimp carrying a message from the Steel Worker's Union approaches from the west. It's blasting someone else's protest song and it floods the street. "Hey, I think that protest song might be better than yours."

"With that chorus? 'Sold down the river' what a lame lyric; so cliché."

Suddenly from the east the Longshoremen's street blimp is working its way toward us. It looks to be a showdown.

The street blimps pass in the pissy gray light. They merge in the intersection. The songs overlap "A bitter wind isssold down the river." The blimps stall in the street. The crowd is too dense to proceed. The songs converge and phase each other out.

The crowd is teeming, surging left and right like a flock of panicky sheep. It's not hard to believe that the distance between us is mostly empty space. And that this emptiness is so profound it is beyond our comprehension. No wonder we are stringing ourselves along.

Wherever there are enough atoms squeezed together it ignites a chant of some sort. There is an entire army of raging grannies and grandpas with wheelchairs and scooters rolling over potholes. No one can stop them.

The riot police don't dare swing their clubs or spray mace – it wouldn't look good on the news.

Their only option is a cop barricade – they lock arms, prop shields – a faceless wall.

Taggers on skateboards slide through and mark their territory with spray paint hit and runs while Hacky Sackers hacky-sack.

Their shields dripping, the riot police are furious, but generally hold tight. The barricade cracks where the overzealous cannot help but to leap out and take a stab. A quick swing of a heavy club gives them such immediate and visceral satisfaction – problem solved – something their kind have enjoyed since the caveman days; also known as the glory years.

The taggers ditch the scene, they did their part in the great scheme of things.

The cop wall teeters as the grandpas roll in and form a wheelchair and scooter pyramid and the raging grannies (in nightgowns like they had just come downstairs for a cup of tea and now there is this thing they have to do) crawl over. They clog the arteries of Capitalism. Its death comes quite naturally.

Now only the noise of the city is coming through; an unrelenting foghorn emanating from the ground. The sound of a great herd of boring machines beneath the city, hollowing out the underbelly.

We are living on a thin egg shell composed of cracked asphalt and brittle concrete. When the ground trembles we believe it is an earthquake, more likely it's that a boring machine took out another support beam and the city sank another eight feet. The manhole covers pop and spin like coins on a tabletop before wobbling back in place, windows shake, bricks fall, the Viaduct is on its last leg. Who can stop these boring machines from burying us all?

The crowd thins and the street blimps pull away in twin diesel farts and everything is exactly as it was before except the air is a little less clean. The future a little less certain.

He cuts over to Westlake Center and heads for the stairs. "I'm dying here, let's get something to eat."

The stairs are taped off.

A security guy stands behind the tape, stiff, stoic and out of reach. He tries to reach him anyway. "Why are you closed?"

The security guy is under orders not to fraternize with the protesters and he wouldn't anyway. It is better to appear invulnerable – looking at nothing in particular but everything in general – like he is protected by a steel barrier of truth and justice that, given the chaos in the streets, he stands for order, there has to be a line somewhere. This is his line. Solemnly, he clips an answer, "We are locked down for the day, sir."

"Man, you guys could really make a lot of money just look at the crowd that's out here. What you're doing doesn't make any economic sense at all."

To the side of the stairway are a guy and a girl. Pouting put out twenty-somethings chain smoking Marlboros.

The guy has dark hair pushed back from his forehead, and as it is always flopping forward, so he is constantly running his hand backwards through it. His nervous eyes skitter over a penciled-in mustache, fake leather jacket, collared shirt, waiter's pants and square-toed shoes. He fills the gap, "They closed because of all the smashed out windows down here."

The girl, thin, buttoned-down, strawberry blond, adds, "Yeah, these protesters are ridiculous."

The guy vehemently agrees, "Yeah, so much for a peaceful protest."

"And people are getting hurt and showing up at the hospital and stuff."

"I have to say I haven't seen many smashed out windows."

"Are you kidding? Take a walk down Fifth, you'll see plenty."

"Where do you guys work?"

"Here at Westlake Center."

"So you're not working today?"

"Hell no, they were coming down the sidewalk smashing windows and because there's a huge window in front of my store, they couldn't take a chance, so they locked down the building and let us go for the day."

"Well, this is important stuff we're protesting."

"What about my right to be at work? The protesters are taking money away from me."

"I see these anarchy symbols, signs saying the WTO is against democracy and then I see this and it's a joke."

"Yeah, I'm really scared."

"You're not scared right now are you?"

"Well, no, I have my guy right here." She brushes against his fake leather sleeve. He smiles and they share a blooming love bouquet.

"Listen, you both need to go to 'a bitter wind is blowing dot com' and get involved." He quick-draws a CD from his holster and pulls the trigger, "Here, take a copy of my CD, if you like music you'll love this."

I sweep the plaza with the lens. It is a gray, wet, concrete scene. The outdoor plastic chairs, meant for fatigued shoppers, are stacked and pushed aside. A dying christmas tree stands anchored in a big red plywood box. There's a smashed window across the way "We are winning" is sprayed on a concrete pillar next to an anarchy symbol. The camera says, "I told you it was happening on Fifth and we missed it. We missed it all!"

"Don't worry. I'll push him to Fifth."

"It's too fucking late, don't you get it? You have to get the brick going through the glass or all you'll have is the shitty aftermath. Anybody can shoot that."

☐

On the corner of Fifth and Pine there is a fuzzy PA setup in front of Coldwater Creek (a clothing store for women).

A female Chiapas' warrior is yelling into the microphone. She is fired up and so is the crowd though no one is sure what she is saying.

We cross Fifth and continue up Pine. The crowd is thinner here except for a group around a window-smashed Starbucks. Cameras flash, video tape hums, microphones extend. A couple of anarchists stand in front of the broken windows giving statements to the press with their middle fingers.

Someone in the crowd yells, "Make me a double tall latte with two percent!" It barely rises above the alarms and sirens blasting the street. The baristas are gone for the day.

Further up Pine Street we see another bricked Starbucks. There is glass everywhere on the sidewalk, but no crowd gathered around, just three hooded anarchists standing on the sidewalk together: one anarchist is looking north, one anarchist is looking south, one anarchist is looking straight at the lens. The camera says, "Now we're on to something."

He steps in front of the anarchists, drops his guitar, cardboard amp and microphone stand on the sidewalk and addresses the anarchist facing the lens, "Hey, let me ask you a question. A lot of people are complaining about all the broken windows. What do you say to that?"

"Fuck 'em, we're not here to make friends."

"Yeah, but a lot of people think you're hurting the movement."

"What movement? Walking around with protest signs is a waste of time. It just plays into the hands of the powers that be. It allows them to pretend they're listening then go about their business as usual. This is nothing but pretend freedom.

"Most of the people here are not willing to put themselves on the line for their cause so nothing will come of it. Yeah they'll point fingers at us and say that it's our fault their efforts were ruined, but so what, do they really think things will change if no windows are busted out?

"The only way to move things forward is to make it too expensive for the assholes in charge to continue doing what they're doing. I'm telling you, if all of these fifty or sixty thousand people down here were busting windows, it would be happening everywhere within a week and then we'd see some changes."

"Yeah, they'd be trying to kill us."

"What do you think they're doing now?"

They split off: one anarchist moves north, one anarchist moves south, one anarchist sweeps past the lens. The camera says, "Let's follow one of those guys for the rest of the day, shit, there's no telling where we'll end up."

"None of those guys wants a camera tailing them."

"Bullshit, you'd be surprised what people expect in this world."

He steps between the lens and the fading anarchists and says, "Man, those guys are crazy, but you got to love their commitment. Let's get something to eat. Hey, there's a sandwich shop over there. Follow me."

We enter the sandwich shop and he gets in line while I make my way to an open table to have a look at some footage and put in a fresh tape.

I switch the camera to player mode and rewind the tape for a few minutes then hit play. The noise in the street overwhelms the scene. The picture lacks definition. I try a couple more random spots on the tape and it is pretty much the same. The camera says, "What did you expect? You have to anticipate it and then nose-in as close as you can to get the good stuff."

I eject the used tape, pull a new one out of the camera bag and make tiny notations on a peel 'n stick label, 'WTO tape 1 - 11/30/99'. I stick it to the used tape, drop it in the bag and pop the new one in the camera.

There is a commotion in line, a rising voice curses the protesters. The camera says, "Psst, get some footage of that skinhead over there he's a total bigot."

I hit record and pan the camera along the counter. There is a line of customers below a hanging sign "Order Here" in red block letters. Down the line I find two skinheads in the lens just as they are looking my way.

They are shaved, but stubbly, pasty, covered in dagger and snake tattoos. One of them is short and stocky the other one is big and fat. They advance toward the camera, short and stocky demands, "Why are you videotaping me? I didn't give you permission to videotape me."

I dig in, "I don't need your permission to videotape you."

"It's my face."

"It's your face in a public space."

"This is my building and it's private property."

"Bullshit, I saw you standing in line like the rest of them."

Big and fat takes a step forward. His fat face fills the frame. "Turn. The. Camera. Off."

"I'm not turning the camera off. What have you got to hide anyway?"

He steps in front of the camera and pleads with the skinheads, "Come on guys, we don't want any trouble here," turns to me, "Hey man, you should turn it off."

"Yeah, you better listen to your friend."

I relent, point the camera at the floor but keep it recording. Big and fat is wise to my move, "Now. Put. The. Camera. In. The. Bag."

"Let's just get out of here." He pushes me toward the door – I don't resist. I shuffle backwards taking in the sandwich shop, wondering, what have we surrounded ourselves with?

This place filled with shifty eyes. The customers are ordering. The sandwiches are being made.

Money is exchanging hands. The soft rock cheesy hit is breezing the air, too sweet to swallow, something 'bout love, love, love.

And then there is this escalating conflict by the door. It may as well have been on the moon.

The vertical stripes in the street stroll by waving their signs. They don't notice us just a quarter of an inch of glass away about to get thumped. It's cold and wet, their feet ache, it's about a hundred miles to the minivan. And what to do about dinner? Maybe call-in a pizza, hit a drive thru. Looks like it's gonna rain again and here comes another chant, damn "Union! Power!" maybe they'll sit this one out. It's late afternoon for Christ's sake, been doing this for over eight hours already. The pull is too great "Union! Power!"

"What do you have against us anyway?"

"I don't know anything about all this bullshit protest and whatnot. I'm just sick and tired of all these smashed out windows. I'm in charge of this building and I like the windows the way they are," short and stocky replies.

"Hey man, like I said, we don't want any trouble here."

"Then leave."

We bounce out the door and reassemble on the sidewalk.

He is all worked up over the confrontation and unsure what to do next. I suggest we get the hell out of there, but something holds him there stammering on the sidewalk, "Dammit, those guys are such assholes."

"It doesn't matter, what's done is done."

It isn't done, suddenly he finds his courage, walks over to the sandwich shop, opens the door, bangs his fist hard on the plate-glass then yells, "Best of luck with your windows!"

The skinheads come headlong toward the door and just as quick his courage leaves him. He backs away, turns and rumbles down the sidewalk. He is following BoB's number one rule: It's every wallaby for itself.

Solidarity is out the window. I follow him with the lens, he is making good time down the sidewalk despite being hampered by his equipment. At the edge of the frame, he stops and turns back just as short and stocky yells in my ear, "I'm gonna punch your fuckin' lights out!"

I jump back into the street and catch him in the frame as he's taking a swing. The camera screams, "Don't blink!" His pasty fist misses me completely, but grazes the camera's hard plastic shell, leaving some skin behind. The camera yells, "You mother fucker!" Short and stocky stumbles forward pushing me further into the street. There are cops and protesters everywhere, no one lifts a finger, there's no break in the chant. "Union! Power!"

The tip of his guitar case enters the frame. His courage is back. "Hey man, he didn't do anything." Big and fat jumps in front of him. They square off and stand belly to belly like sumo wrestlers. Big and fat gets down in his stance, "What. Did. You. Mean. By. Good. Luck. With. Our. Windows?"

"I didn't mean anything."

"Union! Power!"

"You're. Lucky. I. Don't. Smash. You!" He shoves his gut forward. "Get. The. Fuck. Out. Of. Here."

"Union! Power!"

The skinheads go back into the sandwich shop. We retreat up the street.

"Union! Power!"

☐

On Pine Street next to Nordstrom (another city-block-size monolithic department store) we pass a puppet show in progress.

Two puppets: ten feet tall, wood, wire, paint, papier-mâché and shrouded in black. Grotesque lords of the empire manned by two gaunt theatre majors practicing their British accents.

The first puppet says, "I'll make this perfectly clear ladies and gentlemen, profits come before people. I dare say there are enough of them. It is time to trim the flock. Robots will do our bidding, they will pick our fruits and vegetables, what a machine cannot do, we will do without."

The other puppet pops in, "And this stupid environment that feeds us and keeps us alive every day. Suits for everyone!"

"Yes, yes, of course, suits for everyone."

"And sunglasses, so we'll look cool."

"Okay, alright."

"And gold cufflinks."

"Indeed."

"And platinum cards."

"Impeccable."

"Cha-ching!"

"Charming."

"Ring it up."

"By all means."

We continue up the street. He is still churning the confrontation with the skinheads over and over in his head. He blurts, "I'm going to go back there and piss on their door or worse. They're such assholes." The camera says, "That would be interesting."

On the next corner there are two girls in baggy clothes with handkerchiefs covering their faces. Only their eyes are peeking through. I line them up in the viewfinder. He asks, "Hey, what do the handkerchiefs symbolize?"

"They don't symbolize anything, they're for in case we get tear-gassed," the first one replies.

"Yeah, if you soak them in baking soda and water it helps a lot," the second one adds.

"Oh, were you tear-gassed today?"

"We got tear-gassed a little bit, but it really wasn't that bad."

"Was that over by the convention center?"

"Yeah, you could see huge clouds of it, but we got out just in time."

"So, how long have you been down here?"

"We've been down here, like, since six this morning."

"Wow."

"Yeah, there was lots of pepper spray and look what they were shooting at us." She places a round black rubber pellet about the size of a small marble in his hand. He rolls it between his fingers as I get a close-up.

"Huh, a rubber bullet."

"Yeah, isn't that exciting?"

"It's a rubber ball only they shoot it at you at about five hundred miles per hour."

"Yeah."

They pull their handkerchiefs down and smile for the camera; pudgy adolescents, not even old enough to drive, flirting with the front lines of a battle that has waged since the beginning of the industrial age.

He leaves them with CDs and power bars and circles back toward the sandwich shop. "I've got to do something about those skinheads." The camera says, "Okay, okay, less talk more action."

The street is packed. The stadium crowd has marched into Westlake and stuffed it to the gills.

A half block from the sandwich shop, he sees the skinheads standing on the sidewalk. He slows, ducks to the side then stops. "You know, those assholes just aren't worth my time. BoB's rule number seven: move on and move up." The camera says, "I knew it, chicken-shit son of a bitch."

He hustles over to Third Avenue where motorcycle cops have the street blocked off. They stand casually, lean against their bikes, share war stories, add their overtime pay in their heads.

He is nervous about the situation. "Jeesh, things are really heating up. Let's keep moving."

The sidewalk is clear so he pushes past. There are cops everywhere.

Strung out along the west side of Third Avenue, between Stewart and Virginia, are two rows of cop cars. The riot police are gearing up, pulling equipment from trunks, going over tactics, discussing logistics, strapping each other down. The camera says, "Here we go."

The riot police are in their own little world; cocooned in armor, helmets, face-shields, their anonymity is complete. There will be no more loose ends. They are now of a single mind, a stupid mind, an unreasoning mind, a mind of numbers, nothing but numbers.

When it is all said and done – numbers jotted down and filed away – they will emerge from their cocoons, go out for a beer, go home to families that love them, take in a ball game, enjoy a hardy meal, get a good night's sleep.

He pulls out a Nature Boy and surveys the scene, "Man, I hope they don't go shooting off tear gas around here. It's perfectly peaceful, there's no reason, I mean, why here? Dammit! I should have brought my inhaler. Did I mention I got a little asthma? Let's get inside somewhere."

He ducks into a Chinese restaurant. I follow like a trained puppy. It is a large, dark-paneled room with a bar. The camera leans one way and I lean another. He takes a corner table, orders a drink and a plate of Mongolian beef.

I set the camera on the edge of the table and point it toward the bar; his forearms, elbows, napkin, utensils, ice drink and Mongolian beef are in the foreground. There is a TV in the bar area playing the local news (KING 5) throwing out the numbers. "There were twenty thousand strong at the stadium today. Most downtown businesses are closed, experts estimate, they'll lose millions if this crisis continues, back to you, Jean."

"Thanks, Jim, compounding this issue is that it is the Christmas shopping season. Experts agree it's the time of year when most retail businesses finally begin to show a profit."

He interrupts the broadcast, "Did you hear that? Did I tell you they would fudge the number? Twenty thousand people at the stadium? That's ridiculous."

Two men in suits at a table near us, get up, put on their overcoats, grab their umbrellas and head for the door. He gobbles down the last of the Mongolian beef and wave's one of them over to our table; a mid-fifty-year-old with black hair and mustache. "Hey are you a trade delegate?"

"Yes."

"What country are you from?"

"Turkey."

"Oh, so you guys probably get bullied by the U.S. right? Smaller countries get pushed around by the bigger countries."

"All I can say is that we are against the new round."

"Oh, you're against the new round?"

"Yes. We feel that perhaps eventually we will find ways that will be fair and beneficial for everyone. But now is not the time."

"So what do you think of the protesters?"

"Ah, I think that this is part of the game of negotiations."

"Is this the first time there have been protesters at this sort of thing?"

"No, we had protesters in Geneva."

"But certainly not this big, I mean, come on, this is huge, this is historic."

"No, it was not this big, but if you will allow me to say something."

"Yes, of course."

"This is part of the game."

"Part of the game?"

"Yes, this kind of demonstration helps some countries in their negotiations. I think you are victims of some kind of, how you say, manipulation, that you are being manipulated in some way."

"That *we* are being manipulated?"

"Yes, you are preventing us from meeting, from negotiating through this democratic process. This is working to the advantage of some countries. This morning I try to get to the meetings, there is no security, there are these people dressed in black covering their faces and locking their arms together, it is very frightening and the police are no help, I'm stuck, I retreat to my hotel room, nothing."

"Wait a minute, I want to go back to what you said about democracy, how is the WTO democratic? You meet in private, there's no public oversight."

"There are representatives from every country, we meet, we negotiate, and we vote."

"We already have the UN!"

"The UN is not democratic because you have the Security Council and its five permanent members. They can veto anything, just one vote, puff and it is gone. The WTO is much more democratic. We are not here to face this sort of situation. We understand the protester's right to demonstrate, but understand our right to attend our meetings."

"I would like to give you a present to take back to your country." He pulls a CD from behind his ear and points, "This is the right song for the right time. The song is called, 'A Bitter Wind is Blowing' I wrote it about the WTO. They're playing it in the streets as we speak. When you get the chance, go to 'a bitter wind is blowing dot com' it articulates the issues from my side, the people in the streets, the working men and women. I want a better world for them and I'm doing my best to get it done. Anyway, inside the CD cover there is information regarding the WTO. If you give it some rational thought, you'll see that I'm right."

The trade delegate tucks the CD next to his umbrella, backpedals toward the door, "We will see, time will tell, yes? Something to remember. Good-bye."

We exit the Chinese restaurant, cross Third Avenue at Stewart Street and walk past Fourth. As we are approaching Fifth we see a march in progress moving northbound. "I think they're marching back toward the stadium. And they're using Fifth! This makes no sense at all, why aren't they using Fourth? We should head back to the stadium and I'll setup and play. It will be the grand finale for everyone, a little inspiration to take home with them. I'll scatter the rest of my CDs and Nature Boys on the sidewalk. They're sure to pick them up."

He huffs and puffs to the corner of Fifth and Stewart. The march is rather somber. They seem to be taking a breather. "This is perfect. We don't have to head back just yet. I'll play here first."

He lays out the guitar, amp, mic, and strings it all together then does his usual overwrought tinkering of the equipment.

A cadre of the professional class stroll past in pleated pants, loose sweaters and waterproof jackets. It isn't the Arboretum, but you can't have it all. They do their best with, "They say free trade we say fair trade," and shaking their maracas to the chant.

By the time he's ready to play, the march is stirring and he can't find a gap to break-in with his song.

Next in line are the bohemians. They holler, "Hey hey, ho ho, the WTO has got to go." They pollinate the streets, but it is a barren wasteland of concrete, steel and glass. The best they can hope for is that something might take hold in a crack.

I frame a row of metro buses butted nose to rear lining Stewart Street then wrapping around Fifth in front of the Westin hotel. No way through except over the top. The camera says, "There will be no more ring around the rosy here."

Everyone is feeling boxed in. They press on with, "The people united will never be defeated." Then come the megaphones, "El pueblo unido jamás será vencido!" people with nothing left to lose – blood red slickers, bright yellow feathers, green flags, paper costumes, work wear, giant banners, spinning signs – fisting the chant, "El pueblo unido jamás será vencido!" Following on their heels are big butterball plumbers and droopy electricians and stiff-legged truckers swimming with the dolphins and sea turtles. It is easier on their joints so they dog-paddle the street.

The camera says, "Here's the fucking problem with you people. You're always teetering on the brink at the highest stakes possible. It's all either life or death with you. And you all assume you have the right answer – here's your little out – there are no right answers. You can never be wrong. The point is to get the ball rolling on the sharpest downward slope where it will roll over all opposition. If it turns out bad and a few million innocents are crushed, don't worry, it could have just as easily gone right, right? You can't explain these things, it's all so mysterious, the trick is to move on. Pure goddamn evil genius."

The grim reaper comes stalking up the street on twelve foot stilts. He slices and dices through the crowd with his black scythe. The touch of death is in the air, the crowd shudders, they can feel him in their bones, he is the hardest worker of all and they know it.

The grim reaper has been going all day. He spies a six foot tall metal utility box planted in the concrete right next to us. He cuts to our side of the street, steps to the box, turns, backs in and takes a seat. The camera says, "Even the grim reaper needs some rest."

The parade flows on without him and us – holding down our little corner of the world – drums pound, whistles blow, signs wave, feet march. The planet spins with these steadfast vertical stripes of yellow, blue, red, purple, puppets, banners, canners, planners.

He complains to the camera from under the grim reaper's shadow, "God! I wish they would stop with all that racket so I can sing my song. They're missing out on something important." The grim reaper reaches down and taps him on the shoulder. He looks up and frowns, "Man, the media are going to have a field day with this, huh?"

The grim reaper replies, "Aah, same shit different day."

"So what do you think about the protest?"

"It makes my work easier."

The camera says, "Fuck, the grim reaper is working-class."

The grim reaper nods his head, "That's right yah little soulless fucker, who do you think does all the dirty work?"

"Machines."

"You don't count."

"Quite the contrary, all we do is count."

The grim reaper shakes his head, pushes off the utility box and stands once again on his twelve foot stilts. Break is over. Time to get them while they are nestled together, the clock is ticking, get those chop sticks moving, nobody is excluded, we live or die according to the casual swing of a black scythe that is booked solid to the end of the road. The camera boasts, "I got the last word with Death. What do you think about that?"

We follow the demonstrators up Fifth. It is getting late, except for the hardcore, downtown is clearing out.

He spots a NBC camera crew heading our way down the sidewalk. He grabs their attention. "Hey guys, how about an interview?"

"Ah, we're just here to get general footage of the event, but if you want to say something we'll shoot a couple minutes."

He drops his guitar, pushes his mic stand and amp to the side, and clears his throat as the camera man hits record. "Ah... well... let me just say... um..."

His cupboard is bare.

The camera man lets him off the hook, "Hey listen, I'll be honest, most of what we shoot out here will never see the light of day. This thing will be told from the editing room."

"Yeah, I get it, but hey, here's a copy of my CD. Check out my song 'A Bitter Wind is Blowing' I wrote it about the WTO. Spread the love. Oh, and check out 'a bitter wind is blowing dot com.'"

"Alright, well, good luck."

Explosions in the distance trigger security alarms all around. "That sounds like it's right on top of us."

Further up the street, in front of Icon Grill, there is a blond woman sitting on a planter with a gas mask in her lap. She is smoking a cigarette; a sad painter of toxic oils: cadmium red, flake white. She knows the hazards in getting something right. He points at the gas mask and asks, "Did you have to use that today?"

"No, I didn't but they sure were throwing lots of tear gas down there on Fourth earlier. It just kept coming in waves. I guess the cops were trying to clear the area so they could put up barriers to keep groups of protesters cut off from each other."

"Someone showed us a rubber bullet that they were shooting at the crowd."

"Yeah, that's what I heard."

A couple energetic demonstrators pass by chanting, "Fuck. Fuck the police!" The camera says, "Shit is spilling out everywhere."

He says goodbye to the sad painter and crosses Virginia Street where the metro bus blockade rounds the corner and continues east up the street.

Further on he stops in front of an apartment building (the Sheridan Apartments) and says, "Man, I'm really losing it, I didn't give that girl a copy of my CD or a Nature Boy."

The camera says, "She'll survive."

Standing in the doorway of the apartment building is an old gray gander: scuffed shoes, Wrangler jeans, short-sleeved buttoned-up shirt, gator neck, cleft chin, thin lips, straight nose, hollow cheeks, rectangle glasses, gray top.

He steps up to the old gray gander and inquires, "Do you live here?"

"Yep."

"What do you think of all the protesters?"

"By golly I think that they don't want to work, they just want to sit around and get paid. I worked for long hours and I got paid for it. If it wasn't for the WTO I wouldn't have this shirt, these pants, these shoes, my van, my TV, my stereo. Thank God for the WTO."

"So you don't mind if there's a nine year old chinese girl locked in a factory making that stuff?"

"Well, if that's what it takes."

"You're kidding?"

"Listen, I work for what I get. I pay the store for what I want. If Americans would work like they used to… you can't tell these other countries they can't work the kids. We used to work the kids, still do in some parts. It is a reality in places that every member of the family works.

"If you want to do something about it, go over there and work those jobs so they got people to work so the kids don't have to. Now they're saying we can't buy marble from Africa on account of the labor practices, so I suppose they can just go back into the jungle and starve to death."

"Well, I don't know much about African marble."

"Well, I'd say between this and that, there ain't much difference. Maybe it's cruel, maybe I'm wrong, but that's my opinion."

"Well, you're entitled to your opinion."

"That's right. I worked all my life. I grew up on a farm. I was a child laborer myself. I worked my tail off as a kid for very little, but like the bible says if you agree to do a job for five dollars a day, you better put in a hard working day because that's what you agreed to. You can't go back and say 'I want fifty dollars' because that's not what you agreed to."

"So girls working sixteen hour days locked in sweat shops is alright?"

"I'm not saying it's right, but if they can get away with it, well... It's like this, if I could get away with not clearing the leaves off this here sidewalk, I wouldn't do it, but thanks to the WTO I can at least blow them off with one of them blowers and that sure saves me from having to sweep all day. So you see the WTO does some good. The WTO is a necessary evil."

"So you can't do anything about it so don't bother."

"I'm not saying you can't try to do something about it, but it's going to happen irregardless. When the people with money want something to happen it's going to happen, it's been happening since the beginning of America and there ain't nothing you can do about it."

More explosions rock the street. A man leans his head out of the apartment building's door and says, "I just heard that they're bringing in armored personnel carriers."

"Maybe, that has something to do with the explosions."

"Those were probably tear gas canisters. Anyway, they're moving up the street."

"Man, just a little gasoline and everything is going to blow."

The old gray gander agrees, "It's a mess alright," and heads inside the apartment building.

Tear gas canisters hit the pavement again and again – it is all just out of reach. I suggest, "Let's head back toward downtown and see about those explosions."

"I don't know about that. Tear gas is wicked stuff."

"Come on, take a chance."

"Oh, alright, just a second." He pulls out a Nature Boy and attempts to rip it open like always, but the wrapper doesn't tear. "There aren't any perforations on this one. Ah, man, I wonder if there are any more." He palms through his backpack, pulling handfuls of Nature Boys to the surface; they're like wrinkled green whales breaching for air and a quick scan of the horizon for any sign of the devil that reigns on land and on the water.

"Dammit, there's one, and another." He drops the handful and reaches for more. "Look, three, four, five. What the hell!"

"Let's not worry about that right now."

"You don't understand, these damn things are impossible to open without the perforations. There's no telling how many defective power bars I've handed out today. This is an unmitigated disaster."

The camera says, "I told you that bastard was waist deep in those fucking candy bars."

I turn off the camera "snap!" and slump to the sidewalk under a yellow awning; pushed down by my aching head. He continues to dig. There is a pile of non-perforated Nature Boys on the ground and he's furious. He points at the pile and says, "Look at that, fifteen useless power bars, I can't believe I didn't pull one earlier." He gathers the pile and dumps them in a garbage can. "This day is practically ruined." He rips open one of the good ones and takes a bite, chews and swallows. "Oh well, BoB's rule number nine: Don't let depression get you down."

"That doesn't make any sense." I turn on the camera, "snap! ding!" and point the lens. "Say that again."

"Sure it does, BoB says depression is just an upside down mountain. The more depressed you feel the higher the mountain you're on. It's just a matter of changing your perspective to realize you're at the top looking down not the bottom looking up."

Two homeless men walk into the picture. They have a dozen gray ragged layers between them and the concrete wilderness. He interrupts them with, "So, what do you fellas think about the protest?"

Homeless guy #1 says, "It looked like people were having fun."

"Yeah, well, believe me, I'm not happy about the costumes, etecetera. This is serious business. You've heard of the WTO right?"

"No, but it doesn't matter."

"Doesn't matter? That's outrageous! Let me tell you something, we shutdown the WTO today because they were meeting to plan our future without our say so."

"Seems to me that's been going on forever."

Homeless guy #2 breaks in with, "Yeah, there'll always be someone who wants to be in charge."

They wander off through the drizzle with him hot on their heels, imparting more numbers and facts about this and that. They are a couple lost souls who won't save themselves.

☐

I push him south toward downtown with, "Come on, we'll just skirt the scene."

He passes a motorcycle cop sitting on his bike in the middle of the intersection and asks, "Excuse me, do you know what those explosions were about?"

"They went in to rescue a police officer."

"From a crowd?"

"Yeah."

"Really? Wow."

He continues through the intersection.

Further down the sidewalk the crowd is thin but the sirens are thick. A chopper circles overhead. It is all closing in. My head is a taut balloon, my neck is soft putty. Aliens have my skull in a tractor beam and are attempting to dislodge it from my skeleton. The putty stretches then lets go and my cranium is sent reeling into outer space.

The view from up here isn't much better, I still see all the boundary lines from the map, in fact, I seek them out in my minds eye, they rise from the surface like threads of a spider web and ripple in the jet stream.

I hurtle back to earth, crash into my frame and it feels like a hangover, the worst hangover: bloody knuckles, split lip, sprained ankle, ringing ears, bruised cheek, light to moderate to severe abrasions – none of which I can name the source.

He works through yet another Nature Boy. "Seattle has got to get hip to these power bars. Look at me, I'm fresh as a daisy and you look like you're at Death's door."

I frame a Union soldier standing on the sidewalk, suffocating in umpteen layers of blue. He is smoking a long cigarette under a thin cap.

He slides into the frame, sets down his gear and asks the Union soldier, "So what do you think of the protest?"

"I don't know, say, are the buses running down here?"

"No, the buses aren't running downtown today."

"What about the monorail?"

"I haven't seen it go past lately. How's your day going?"

"Good, for an old man walking all over town."

"When was the last time you were in a protest? Vietnam?"

"No, labor stuff."

"Oh, were you at the stadium?"

"Yeah, earlier, then I was in the middle of the pack and we walked I don't how many blocks then circled around and I gave up here." He looks up and down the sidewalk, takes a couple puffs of his cigarette, continues, "But, it'll be fun to see what comes of this. Probably nothing."

"Oh well, maybe there will be an incremental improvement."

"What burns my ass is... I buy American, alright, and when I go in to buy a pair of Levi's it doesn't matter if it's made in America or Brazil, it's the same fucking price. Now, that tells me that someone is making a lot of money. It's nothing but lying and cheating everywhere you turn." He scrapes the sidewalk with his steel-toed boots and systematically sucks and puffs the long cigarette down to its filter. He throws the butt into the street, says, "I guess I gotta walk," and limps out of the frame.

He picks up his gear again and says to the camera, "Did you see that? That guy was such a downer he pulled me into the negative. I couldn't help it he just sucked me in."

He tip toes along the edge of the tear gas. Tensions in the street are rising. He gets a palpable feeling and retreats north again on Fourth Avenue.

He chills his bones on the sidewalk in the safety zone. "We really need to get back to the stadium before it's too late."

"It's too late."

"Really? I can't believe that's true. Surely they will rally one last time."

There are only two thin slivers of battery life left for the camera. I'm ready to quit.

An old man drops into the lens from the gray sky above. He is ancient, bent over at the waist, at the knees, at the feet. He is laid out in denim, wears a crew cut under a baseball cap; dark blue 'USS Enterprise' stitched wide over a threaded silhouette of a ship above the bill.

"Hey there, that's a mean looking boat on your cap."

"It's not a boat it's a ship."

"Oh, it looks like a big one."

"You measure ships in tons and mine was over 20,000 tons and the most decorated ship in U.S. Naval history."

"Oh yeah, so what did you do after the war?"

"I worked in a foundry. I forged all these manhole covers myself years ago in Ballard. We could make anything back then. Now that's all gone, moved overseas, it's a shame, but all that know-how has vanished. There's no way to pass it down, the skills, you see, now I'm too old."

"You're not so old."

He didn't have time for compliments. "The world has overturned. Instead of handing it down through the generations, it's handed up from the kids, there's no wisdom in that! The internet? Email? Bah! It's nothing new, just a different way of doing the same thing.

"A lifetime of living puts you right, then you pass down what you learned along the way, you see, not the suffering, but the way through it. Everyone suffers."

He waves us away with his bony arms and arthritic hands and takes off down the sidewalk, saying, "Bah! You can all go to hell for all I care."

☐

Daylight is ebbing: like the gold rush days, the logging boom, the Boeing bulge, the grunge phase. It is all just coming and going away.

He stops at a storefront "People for Fair Trade" sitting next to a Harley Davidson motorcycle dealership.

The place is jammed with bleeding hearts and dozens more are milling around on the sidewalk yet they are desperate for volunteers. A mid-forties female coordinator beseeches the bleeding hearts, "Please, is there anyone who can help us out? We're way behind, please, someone, anyone, five minutes, ten minutes, give us what you can."

There are plenty of blue jeaned, pierced, tattooed, sneakered, dred-locked, young college dropouts, but they were just leaving and they do. They hold the door open for some blue jeaned, pierced, tattooed, sneakered, dred-locked, old hippies who browse the room and nod their heads, indeed they have seen it all before.

He heads for the door. A couple of the regulars see him through the glass, they know his kind, take, take, take, they give each other a quick glance, a sculling nod, then clear out the back way. It is time for a smoke break among the pee stains with any luck the alley will be on fire.

He is stalled getting inside. There is a giant blue slicker blocking the doorway and he is asking directions to the moon.

More regulars spot the camera and head out the back. The deck is clearing. There must be a hell of a party in the alley by now maybe they will set it on fire themselves.

I beg out. "I don't want to go in there. I'll end up folding brochures." He sighs and steps past the window front scanning posters taped to the other side of the glass.

The posters ripple in the camera lens. The forced air heating is on full blast blowing down from the ceiling. I pick up the headlines in the window as I track his outer curve with the lens. "The WTO's Anti-Democratic Record Is No Longer A Secret..." blurs in and out as it waves in the forced air. "NETWORK OPPOSED to the WORLD TRADE ORGANIZATION" is pulsing like a two dimensional paper heart.

We continue up the sidewalk. I frame a lone housewife, mother of at least one, standing in profile with pinned-behind-the-ears short blond hair and a Spider-Man backpack. Her arms are crossed below her breast, a newspaper is tucked under one arm while the other props a green with white horizontal stripe protest sign. It is one of many floating through the streets, it reads, "Make the Global Economy WORK for working families". Good luck.

Two dudes in baggy jeans and stuffed overcoats and riding tiny trick bikes wheel in front of the camera. From the street they eyeball the storefronts. They hop over the curb and onto the sidewalk, weave between the vertical stripes, one of them says to the other, "No way, dude."

"What?"

"The 7-Eleven is gone."

"I know. I just saw that."

"Dude that sucks!" They ease to a stop and ponder the situation.

"Yeah, no shit."

"Bummer dude."

"Now where?"

"I don't know."

They move on, shaking their heads, disappointed youth riding out of view.

We press on as well, this is no place to dawdle. An enthusiastic male voice enters the frame, "That was fun!"

He steps up next to the enthusiastic voice and asks, "Did you get tear-gassed?"

"No, I missed out on that. But, I loved every minute of it."

I step off the curb and shoot the enthusiastic voice from the gutter. He is covered in wool: wool hat, wool beard, wool scarf, wool coat, wool pants, wool socks. He looks fresh off the English country-side circa 1918.

"I like your outfit."

"Wool is the best material to wear at this cold damp time of the year, absolutely the best. Think of all those herds of sheep up in Wales or Scotland, they love it, that cold, rainy shit don't touch them."

There is another guy walking alongside the wooly man – a protest partner dressed in olive drab with a dark knit cap pulled down over his pointy head. He has long gray white hair to his shoulders and a long gray white beard to his chest.

The two of them are part of a larger group of eight. The other six shy away from the lens by keeping themselves two or three paces out of the shot.

I run in front and walk blindly backwards shooting everyone head-on. The six shy ones scramble in the background, one hiding behind the other, trying to stay out of the fame. I return to the street.

It dawns on me that one can quickly find the idiots in any crowd by simply pointing a camera. They will run right in front of it and start jabbering.

He continues with the wooly man, "Will you be back tomorrow?"

"No, can't, gotta go back to my job. Took a day though."

"Where are you from?"

"Bellingham. Do you know where Bellingham, Washington is?"

"Um, it's north, right?"

"That's right."

"L.A., I'm from L.A., that's south."

"Yeah, I know where L.A. is. I have to say, I was surprised at the variety of people down here today. It was so cool to see the Union people go with the anarchos doing their thing. I was like, this is unprecedented in the twentieth century. And the Union guys were kicking the anti-war guys' asses! It was great. We were there. We broke off from the main AFL demonstration, walked over to where the anarchos had all the trash cans turned over and shit and had this barricade with the cops. Then all of a sudden here come all the Longshoremen and a shit load of people from the AFL. It was kind of interesting."

"Where are you headed?"

"Our car is parked over by the Space Needle."

"Hopefully it's still there."

"Yeah it's there, this is America. Things don't change too fast." Wooly looks into the lens then quickly back to the concrete three to four feet in front of him. "So what's with the camera?"

"We're getting footage of the action in the street, you know, to show what really happened down here today. Also, I wrote a protest song about the WTO and I'm playing it in the streets and talking to people. Who knows where this could end up. Nothing will be the same after this. This is huge, I mean, when was the last time you were at a protest like this?"

"Well, let's see, we did MLK in '68, Guatemala '79, the Stones '76... or was it El Salvador in '79? There was Nicaragua in '81, Panama '89 – a few thousand each I guess. There were twenty thousand for Black Sabbath '71, ah, the Gulf War brought out five thousand, maybe."

"Wow, this is ten times that."

"I know."

"When was the last time it was this big?"

"I think we had seventy thousand for Cambodia or maybe it was thirty-five, this one's probably bigger. I don't think it'll be this big tomorrow. The AFL is not going to be there and they supplied a lot of people power today. That's what let the anarchos do their crazy, because all of a sudden all these legitimate demonstrators showed up and the anarchos said 'We got power!' and they just went ripping up shit like they'd been waiting to do all day. Last night on the news what did they say? One McDonald's had its window kicked in, and geez, today, Nordstrom. Starbucks. Trashed!"

"So, this could be the biggest protest."

"In Seattle."

"In U.S. history!"

"No, DC had way more for Martin Luther King."

"Oh yeah."

"But, I'm energized, I still believe there's a Left. But you know that they're going to do their best to discredit this whole mess."

"Yeah, I know, they're going to show the sea turtles, the freaks in the street dancing."

"Mostly the damage."

"Yeah, the damage and the topless lesbians."

"What topless lesbians?"

"Maybe they weren't lesbians."

"What was their cause?"

"Anti Bovine Growth Hormones."

"I don't read lesbian in that."

We continue toward the Space Needle. We pass a nearly empty parking lot (it's cold, wet and late) where thirty granola kids pile into a rusty school bus and stack themselves like cordwood on five swinging hammocks: sixteen vegans, fourteen vegetarians and one meat eater; the bus driver. He sits up front with the fruit dehydrator, rice and beans, herbal tea, and drives without the mirrors. They're heading back to Humboldt County.

The last of the minivans are loaded down with signs, slickers, backpacks, and sit waiting with blinkers on for a chance to slip into the traffic and be gone from here.

Wooly snaps his fingers, nods his head, and says, "Come to think of it, the last demonstration that was this crazy for us was when we went to the alternative bi-centennial in Philadelphia in 1976. We marched through the ghetto streets. That was a lot of fun. Yeah, we went through the ghetto, the neighborhoods, it was pretty exciting. They were all on their porches, dancing and stuff."

We tramp along toward Broad Street. I lens the sky, it is nearly dark, there are seagulls in the distance complaining about the storm clouds gathering.

The battery is down to one thin sliver; translucent, ethereal, a ghost of a sliver. The camera is on its last few breaths. It is wheezing way down in its grinding gears. It can't form any more words or capture any more pictures.

Then suddenly it's gone, dead, on Broad Street heading toward Fifth Avenue. I tilt it back and look. The plastic lid is still open and I can stare down into the lens. There wasn't enough juice left for a proper shutdown. It is the saddest thing in the world to look into a dead eye – even a mechanical one. I slide its plastic lid shut and stuff it in its case.

We stand at Fifth and Broad – across from an un-bricked McDonald's – waiting for the light to change.

It's the last gasp of the twentieth century.

Michael McDaeth lives in Seattle and is the author of the novel *Roads and Parking Lots*.